# Reins of Satan

The reins of Satan are harnessed to the sins of violence.

Civil War veteran Gabriel McDermott has spent the last thirty years as an enforcer for anyone who could pay. But times have changed. It is now 1897 and the Old West is fading. His talents are no longer in demand and this hard man is now seen as a relic from long ago.

In a desire to escape his past and settle down, he turns in his young travelling companion for a $1500 reward. However, when his partner is hanged without a trial, the execution awakes Gabe's lost conscience. Memories from a violent past return to haunt and his nerve fails – just when Satan decides to call.

*By the same author*

Raking Hell
No Coward
The Proclaimers
Reaper

For more information about the author
please visit: www.leeclinton.com

# Reins of Satan

Lee Clinton

**A Black Horse Western**

ROBERT HALE · LONDON

ISBN 978-0-7198-1610-9

Robert Hale Limited
Clerkenwell House
Clerkenwell Green
London EC1R 0HT

www.halebooks.com

Typeset by
Derek Doyle & Associates, Shaw Heath
Printed and bound in Great Britain by
CPI Antony Rowe, Chippenham and Eastbourne

*For Scott M.*
*Who shone a light into the dark.*

# 1

# GENESIS - STAINS

*'You always remember the first man you kill and the last. It's the ones in between that hide in the shadows, only to come out when you least expect.'*

These were the words said to me by my sergeant. I was nineteen and he was twenty-three, and as life weary as my grandfather and then some. He had been at Pittsburg Landing where they could smell the scent of victory through the stench of the dead – but it wasn't to be. I joined just after as a fresh-faced boy soldier along with the other youthful reinforcements, and in just six months we were all battered, brittle, and preparing for our annihila-tion. But that didn't come either. We skirmished south to fight on for nearly three more years. When we abandoned Richmond, our lives had been exhaled to exhaustion. I was now twenty-two, and a sergeant. I was also starting to see the faces in the shadows. They would come during fitful bouts of cold, uncomfortable sleep.

I remembered each last man I had killed, until he became the second last, then the third – dimming in my memory, fourth – fading, fifth – into the gloom, sixth – gone.

The war may have ended, but they hadn't departed. Without warning, they would come back to reappear and stand before me in the half-light of half-sleep, just before dawn, observing me. It was to continue over the years with unrelenting repetition as their faces, never looking any older, multiplied. I would wake with a start, a kick, sometimes a yell, thrashing out of my bedroll. The others in the camp would stay well away and give me ground around the campfire. To the young cowhands I was a curiosity, but in a boarding house, where men crowded in and slept cheek to jowl, I was an embarrassment and someone to steer clear of.

Later, those silent faces from the dark past started to talk. They pleaded to be released and I pleaded with them to go. My only salvation was liquor and work. I worked hard from before dawn to after dark. It was a life around cattle and men, where pride and self-respect had to be earned with fist and gun. And at night I would let the alcohol wash away the memories and bad dreams. But, just like the tale of that final straw upon the camel's back, the weight of my dark thoughts from my nightmares and sins had collected to near breaking point. It was as if the delicate spring of a prized pocket watch was being slowly overwound by its zealous owner.

That was just before Hiram got inside my head and pushed all the others out.

He was a Tennessee boy, some twenty or more years younger than me, from near Thompson's Station. His family name was Miller and he was related, through marriage, to the Tates. These kin were wild and unpredictable but Hiram was different. He could hold his liquor, mouth, and gun steady. He had also been my last and final partner. There would be no more. I had made sure of that.

We were never real close. It was more a partnership of convenience, but we had ridden together and shared profits when they came our way, so that must have counted for something. But even if it didn't, what I did to Hiram Miller saw me sink to a depth of depravity that not even I believed I was capable.

9

I had seen an old poster by chance that said he was wanted in Kansas for horse thieving over near Emporia, from sometime before we had met up. The reward was $1,500, which to me, at my time of life, was a king's ransom. I could never make or save that sort of money in the years I had left. So when we reached Caldwell, I turned him in by having a quiet word with the deputy, who was standing in for the Marshal while he was up in Wichita on law business.

I then went over to the saloon, so that I wouldn't be around when Hiram was arrested at the barbershop while taking a shave. I was told that he went quietly and with a degree of good cheer in the belief that he could prove his innocence. However, he was never to get the opportunity to do so. My foul deed sent him to hell, and in doing so I had woken the devil, who now wanted his next reward – me – and he was going to let Hiram's kin do his bidding.

I had seen men take their own lives when trapped in despair. I had always judged it to be a weak-headed act, and felt no remorse for them or their predicaments. But if only I had shown such character and confronted my sins, while still in Caldwell, and put a gun to my head. Had I, then this sorry story would never need telling, and in doing so, I would have saved a great deal of suffering upon the two most important people that were to ever come into my long life. For my actions and inactions I still seek their forgiveness, while knowing that I can never accept their pardon. Some stains can never be scrubbed clean and this is one.

# 2

# MUD

*Caldwell, Kansas – 1897*

It was that look – a quick look from one eye. That's all I got to see, just that one eye, before the coal black hood was pulled down over Hiram's head, and the large bleached knot of the noose was twisted to the side of his neck. But it was enough. He saw me and he knew who had sold him out. He showed no surprise. There was no look of accusation or cry of denunciation, not even blame. It was as if he expected it – that I would be the one to do him in. His look told me of his resignation and while I showed no sentiment upon my face, inside I felt myself sink to the very depths of wretchedness. For the first time in an age, I sensed shame and looked down – down at the brown-black mud that squelched under my boots as I stood mired, if ready to be sucked into the earth. Oh, how I wished it could have been.

When I looked up, Hiram's head was completely covered, but he stood straight up, tall and soldier-still with no trembling, no sign of fright, just the soft and gentlest shifting of his weight from one foot to the other. I could see where his ankles were bound and the toes of his boots lifted slightly, hardly seen, as he readied to meet his maker.

When the trapdoor whacked open and he shot to earth feet first, I felt my nerve snap with the violent jerk of the rope. But the hangman had failed to do his job and Hiram was thrown back into the air to wriggle, twist and dance. The women in the crowd gasped as one, some bringing both hands to their faces to cover their eyes or clench at flushed cheeks; while the men let out a collective groan as if they were somehow next upon that high scaffold. It was just the juveniles who jeered and laughed, but it was a false show of bravado that went quiet when Hiram finally hung there, motionless at the end of a creaking rope. The observance of this death would come back to haunt each of these boys when they were on their own, away from the collective courage of their childish clans and in their beds. At night, each creak of a floorboard would sound like the hangman's rope or the footsteps of the grim reaper himself.

I'd seen men hung before. I'd hung men before but never with such ceremony. Mine were sordid little affairs of rough and instant justice. I'd even hung an Indian woman in '83 for thieving. The rope broke just as she was hoisted high, but that didn't deter us. We mended the line with tidy knots while she looked on, then pulled her high again. Seeing death up close was commonplace to me, but this time, with Hiram, I felt a new chill snake up my back like someone dragging sharp steel spurs across my naked skin. I knew what it was – it was Satan calling. I was going to hell. My life and times had finally tracked me down and caught me up. I had been the lifetime servant of the devil and now he was calling in his dues.

# 3

## WHY ME?

*Marshal's Office, Caldwell*

'Where's the other $300?' I looked Deputy Marshal Hargraves straight in the eye as I spoke, my face only inches from his.

'That's it. That's all there is.' His tone was cocksure and he was playing to the others in the office, who were within earshot and straining to hear more of our transaction.

'It's supposed to be $1,500, not twelve. Like the poster bill says, $1,500 reward.' I pointed to the wall where the old poster now held pride of place, but he didn't look, he knew. 'This is only twelve.'

'That's it, Gabe. That's what you get and that's all there is. And don't you go running to the mayor squawking. Him and me have an arrangement.'

I should have known, I'd been in and out of Caldwell over the years and those arrangements were long standing. It was no more than honour amongst thieves. My missing $300 would be split between the Marshal's office and the Mayor. Hargraves would hand all the money to the Marshal on his return, who would take his cut and divvy the rest between the two Deputies and the Mayor. I could just see that little, fat, town official receiving his in an envelope, in silence, as he placed it inside his bible. He would then continue on to church to pray for the good people of this border town and for the soul of Hiram – to justify the lynching.

Just a week before, I would have killed any son of a bitch that tried to do what Hargraves was doing to me. But now, it was different and he sensed that I was spent and no longer a danger. It was written on my face and seen in my eyes. I was no longer the man with the mad dog reputation. I glanced around and lowered my voice so that the others couldn't hear. I knew I was acting like a dog with my tail between my legs, and had I pulled my gun and shot him there and then, up close, then kicked him in his wound when he went down, I would have at least got back some self-respect before being gunned down myself. But I didn't. My Colt remained in its leather, a cold iron on my hip with no threat from a once hot-head. What had happened to me?

'You want me to count it out again, Gabe?'

I said nothing. It was all that I was going to get.

I'd already been robbed, so I didn't need to be reminded by a recount of what was left. I just shook my head and picked up the dirty bank notes that had passed through the pockets of the poor and shoved them into my jacket.

'Now sign here.'

The receipt book looked official and alleged that I was signing for $1,500. Hargraves handed me the pen, after he had dipped it into the inkwell. The smell of the ink travelled my mind back to Miss Robbins and my schooling, where I had been taught to read, write and cypher. It was still a most agreeable memory of accomplishment and praise, and had the war not intervened to leave me seeking solitude and consolation at the bottom of a bottle, I could have held a position as a clerk in a bank or with the railroads. I took the pen from the Deputy and held it hard above the signature line and pushed my face close to the paper. I then lifted my head and softened my hold on the stem like I was taught. I ran a line of ink straight through the word *fifteen* and wrote *twelve* directly above. As I finished the word, I let the nib sweep from the last letter and trail to a fine end. I was showing off the style of my hand, seldom used but never forgotten from an early age. I signed and drew the pen across the two Ts of my surname with a flick and dropped the pen back into the inkwell. The point of the nib clinked hard against the glass bottom.

'You son of a. . . ! What have you done, Gabe? Where'd you learn to read and write?'

He pulled the receipt from the book and crushed it tight in his hand, letting the wad drop into the wastebasket. I knew he'd write a new one to suit, but he had to remonstrate, show his authority, his superiority over me. He thought he was such a modern man and that I was old fashioned, from long ago. I had seen it when he used the telephone on the wall and bellowed to the caller on the other end of the line, showing off, showing who was boss. He was that sort of man. I may never have had a conversation on a telephone. I had no need, but my proficiencies in life were more than his could ever be and I'd showed him up. For just a moment, I had revealed that I was above him, so he had to put me down. Put me back in my place like I was some miscreant in his town, but I had once towered over him. It was not just that I could read and write. I had seen and done things that were beyond his mind. I had once been courted by the rich and powerful, and feared by their rivals and enemies. I had also been a soldier and seen the depths of inhumanity that is war. And I had survived.

The hardships and violence of the frontier after '65 were petty to the happenings between the blue and gray. I had seen Federal and rebel alike slaughtered in an artillery hell. I had stood in line, exposed to fire from the flanks and with my bayonet fixed. I had looked into the eyes of my opponent and killed him with neither malice nor remorse. I had been thrown headlong into that depravity with a sense of honour that comes from being called to arms. But it was just the false pride of youth and folly, of new smart uniforms and the looks from girls with a gleam in their eye. It all vanished with the first shot of battle.

I learnt the truth. There is no nobility in death; just the reality of waste and the bloated black corpses of loved ones. For those left behind, it was a lifetime of misery and loss that is empty of meaning, except for a locket of hair by which to remember what might have been.

*Why me, why did I survive? What did God have planned for me?* I had asked over and over again. But he had no plan. God went missing at Antietam and I went west after our final defeat, to avoid the northern saddle of reconstruction and the greed of the carpetbaggers.

'Anyway, Gabe, twelve hundred is more than you'll ever earn or need.' Hargraves was posturing again. 'You'd be lucky to get seventeen cents an hour as a labourer. And you are an old man now. You're fifty or more I reckon, so doing sixty hours of hard employment a week is beyond you.'

It was horseshit, but I wasn't going to argue. I had no notion for it. He didn't know how much I'd been working for. He just wanted to put me down by referring to me as just a hand, but I'd been on a foreman's wage when I provided my services to the respected Mr Allan and buried his enemies.

Hargraves waved a finger at me. 'Now don't you go getting drunk and ornery, Gabe. You just buy your whisky and drink it out of town away from the good folk.'

I put my hat on slowly and slid my fingers across

the brim then drew back the phlegm into my throat. For a moment, he thought I was going to spit on him, but I turned and left, spitting on his porch as I went.

He called after me, angry, 'And you watch your back, McDermott, some people might not be too happy with what you've gone and done.'

I turned, 'What did you say?'

'Some people might find out that you turned your partner in. Like his kinfolk, and they may not take too lightly to that.'

'I may have turned him in, but I didn't hang him.'

'Well, that's the law. Our legislators make the law, and they have brought back capital punishment. It's what the people wanted. I don't make the law, I just enforce it.' His voice was raised in pitch.

'But what about a trial? You were supposed to have a trial first,' I said.

'He was a wanted man, dead or alive, so there was no need. He was guilty.'

'And you call yourself a Christian,' I mocked.

'You leave the good Lord out of this.'

'Looks like that's what you did.' I turned and left. I'd had enough. I could never win this argument, not with a man who had the power to make up the rules as he went. It was a lynching, plain and simple, albeit a legal one and done for public amusement. Had I a price on my head in Kansas, he'd be just as happy to collect the reward and hang me too. Especially as this was an election year, but fortunately my crimes in his State were on the orders of another man, more powerful than the Marshal and the Mayor combined – and they knew it. I spat on the porch again and stepped down into the mud of Main Street.

'You think you're smart, McDermott, but you just watch your back in case someone comes a calling.'

'They'll have to find me first,' I yelled back.

'Oh, they can do that all right, I'll see to it myself.'

It was a none too veiled threat and maybe I should have paid it heed, but I didn't, I just walked on, straight across to the Silver Dollar on the other side of the street. I needed a drink, real bad.

# 4

# IN VAIN HOPE

*Silver Dollar Saloon, Caldwell*

The alcohol burn of corn liquor calmed both my nerves and my anger, for just a while. Then, after half a bottle I felt the meanness come over me. I contemplated going back across the street to settle up, but my head was light and my focus hazy. Fortunately, I had sense enough to stay put. I'd been in a gunfight when drunk, but only once. I should have been killed on that occasion.

I drew quickly and fired my first shot, but my aim was poor and I missed my mark completely. In my

23

drunken state I was most surprised, as I just took for granted that I would have my quarry, but now he had me dead. He took careful aim, as if in a duel, and squeezed the trigger. The click of the hammer was heard by all, when his Navy failed to fire, and in his moment of disbelief, he hesitated to pull back on the hammer and fire that second shot. Instead, he turned, just slightly, and this delay was just long enough for me to raise my Army to eye level and with both hands – steady and fire.

I aimed for his chest and was only twenty paces away, but the shot still went high, punching into his neck, now side-on, instantly gouging out his windpipe and voice box. He dropped his gun and clutched at his throat as he reeled and staggered, but didn't fall. In fright, he went to cry out but couldn't. No words, not even a breath came from his lips. His eyes flashed with dread while I fired a third shot to finish him off and missed completely, that's how drunk I was. This wild volley went into the bar of the Buffalo Head Saloon, scattering the patrons. I believe that bullet mark is still there to this day as a reminder of past rough times.

I also recall that my wounded game went as white as a sheet, and we all stood and watched as air sucked back in through the gaping hole in his neck, then splashed back out in a spray of exhaled blood. The bartender called out to stop, waving a white towel above his head like a flag of truce. He kept looking at me as if for permission as he stepped forwards, then pressed the towel to the victim's throat. It immediately blocked the flow of air. The standing corpse came alive and stamped his feet to signal his distress, so the towel was removed. The air rushed out with squirting blood then sucked back into the hole, flapping the torn skin on his neck.

I holstered my handgun on the third try and could still smell the burnt powder in the air as the bartender escorted the casualty towards the door. He was taken down to the physician, assisted by two patrons and a small band of onlookers, with his open wound exposed to the ordinary people on the street. I stayed in the saloon and had another drink. The story came back, later, that some townsfolk had turned white with shock when they saw the walking wounded with the hole in his neck and its flapping skin.

I learnt my lesson that day never to gunfight drunk. It was a lesson worth learning. The number of drunks I shot dead when I was sober ended up beyond count. Their courage may have been up, but their reflexes were down and slow as they signalled their intentions to do me harm. And when they shot, their aim was always high and off-centre. They were all fools who deserved to die, as I did on that day.

When I stumbled from the Silver Dollar it was dark. I had a mind to leave Caldwell and the likes of Hargraves straight away. But when I got to the livery stables I had trouble opening the stall door I was so inebriated; and as for fitting a saddle to my horse, Star, that would have been an impossibility. So I leant against his smooth, warm belly, then slid down at the gelding's feet and slept the night out.

When I woke it was just on first light. My head hurt real bad and my mouth was as dry as straw. I heard the livery clerk arrive with his banging of his hay rake in the next stall, so I arose on unsteady feet and paid up early. His cheek made it clear that I was looking poor and pitiful as I rolled up my half bottle of Kentucky from the night before into my blanket, and headed off towards the Allan property.

I had no mind to seek work there with Mr Allan as he had no use for me now. He wanted to be free from the past in his bid to become a congressman. I was just passing by his back door towards a place that I had kept in mind for over twenty years. This was my last chance. At last, I had some money to take up land where I could finally mark my own patch to settle down and hide away. But to get there was going to be a ride short on comfort and long in the saddle. This would put distance between me and my past, and keep me safe in a place where my face and reputation were unfamiliar.

If only I had known what lay before me. If I had, then maybe I would have been content to seek solace from a hundred bottles and in the arms of a dozen whores – in the vain hope of a quick death through the excesses of vice and drink. But I did not know, so I rode on in blissful ignorance.

# 5

# FIRE AND ICE

*Heading North-west*

The looks from the townsfolk, as I rode out, made it clear that unforgiving news travels fast. Caldwell's weekly newspaper would write large on Hiram's apprehension and execution, but it was not due out till later that day, so I suspected that the Mayor, who was also the town's self-appointed clergy, had preached from the pulpit at evening prayers of my betrayal. But I bet he never preached to the flock on the injustice of no trial or advised them of his commission from Hargraves. Somehow these two community guardians would reconcile their dishonesty as no more than fair dues for services rendered. Their hypocrisy was as much a sin as my betrayal of Hiram, yet while I felt wretched with remorse, they felt none from their duplicity. What kind of man builds a reputation on righteousness, yet has no virtue in his heart? I may have been involved in despicable acts, but I was an honest broker in my dealings and never sought to lie or hide what I did or what I had become. My heart was bare and cold for all to see.

The ride out past the cemetery led through the old mine diggings. Holes of hope, I had heard them called, that only deferred the inevitable disappointment that accompanies such dreams. I had never met a miner who had struck it rich. It made me doubt if the poor could ever profit through honest effort alone. It seemed to me that all wealth came through corruption and deceit. It was a secret the rich and powerful understood well.

A speculative company was now searching for oil amongst the piles of rubble. These were practical men from Ohio working for contract wages, as they constructed their towers that reminded me of the gallows. A dozen of these wooden scaffolds stood and mocked me. Fortunately, their servants were busy men who paid little attention to local gossip and showed their neutrality by a wave, as if I was just a passing neighbour. I returned the compliment as I rode on. It would be the only goodwill I would receive from this pitiless place.

I headed west across to the tributary, now knee-deep with the early rains that were washing the summer flotsam from the banks, then turned north-west. It was close to midday before I stopped for coffee, upstream where the water was crystal clear. I stripped off my shirt and bathed, taking the time to shave from the leftover hot water from my brew, while Star drank long, walking away from the water's edge to relieve himself, then return for another drink. Of all the horses I had owned over the years, Star was the only one I had ever seen doing such a thing. Where he had learnt such behaviour I didn't know, but it always amused me. I put his good manners down to the gentleman that he was.

I was now travelling light and fast, prepared to spend time in the saddle, which would cause me to purchase provisions as I went. However, this time I now had the means to pay my way, which was a relief. I had rolled the reward money into two bundles each of $500, wrapped them in cloth and tucked one into the empty coffee pot, and the other into a corner pocket of my saddle valise. What was left of the remaining $200 from my hard night's drinking was in my jacket. It alone was more than I had had at any one time over the past few years. This capital now represented my last shot at any comfortable future. It had come at the cost of Hiram's life and that legacy was now beginning to take its toll.

That night in a fitful sleep, a vision of his face appeared up close and could not be shaken from my mind when I awoke. It was as if he had joined me on my ride. This uninvited visit was a reminder that the spending of my putrid purse required careful consideration. These were the wages of sin. I also knew that I would have to stay away from the liquor or I would just waste my bounty, but that was easier said than done.

I made good time to Dodge City, where I picked up some salted beef, flour and a little sugar, then went north to Colby, arriving there before week's end. I purchased some coffee and potatoes at a bloated price from a fat shopkeeper with a red face, who displayed too much interest in my business. I showed my disapproval with sullen silence and headed for Greeley, crossing where the state line meets Nebraska to the north and Colorado to the west. The weather out of Greeley was turning chilly, but not unpleasant. It was, after all, late fall. At Fort Collins, I had a stewed lamb dinner with onions, bought some molasses and had Star reshod, as the blacksmith offered a good deal. The fort's cavalry had gone south and left him with too much spare time on his hands and no cash coming in. I had the money and he was quick and good at his trade.

The next day, I crossed into Wyoming and made for Rawlings and then past the hot springs and on to the Owl Creek Mountains. I had travelled close to 700 miles in less than twenty four days and Hiram had travelled every one of them with me, but I was almost there.

As I headed into the mountains I picked up an old Indian trail, just as a solid wall of black cloud swamped the sun, casting its gloom over the countryside. It was ominous weather with intent to harm, especially when on your own and far from shelter. Star and me needed to get moving if we were to get through the pass before the arrival of the first snows, so I nudged his flanks and he agreed, breaking his stride from a walk into a canter.

I've had more than my share of winters in high

country, and each cold season would arrive to re-acquaint me with its steely meanness. Yet, I always seemed to forget the bite of a past winter's chill. But this time it would be different as no one expected that winter to be so early or fierce, and many were caught out, including me.

That day did not just mark the start of a fierce winter chill with its physical discomfort, but also an alarming dread that came upon my mind. Hiram was now my constant and unwanted companion, appearing in bursts like the flash from a photographer's wand. Then, without warning, I heard him call to me. It sounded like a voice on the wind, as if following behind. Without thought, I turned and said Yes, Hiram. But he wasn't there. This one-way conversation from the saddle spooked Star.

'Steady, old boy,' I said quietly, 'it's only the devil baiting me. He has no quarrel with you.' I pulled off my glove and patted him down, but he didn't believe me, his head twisting to the side. Maybe he knew I'd be happier to see the devil at that moment than I would be to see Hiram. The devil knew my ways well and didn't need an explanation as to my actions, but Hiram did.

I was now getting high up into the mountains, as the wind got stronger and the first light flakes of snow swept through the trees. We edged our way up the steep climb of the trail and two hours later, the first snowfall of the season descended in a blizzard of wild wind and whip cracking lightning. I had been riding through the calm before the storm and had been lulled into an illusion that all would be fine. The sting of the wind upon my face made me consider if I should turn around and head back down, but I was impatient, and even though I knew it was foolishness to keep going, as I was ill-prepared for the journey ahead, I pressed on, telling myself that I was up to it. But, within the hour, self-doubt had taken its grip. I had got myself into a desperate spot and worry now occupied my mind; along with Hiram.

The effort required by Star was indeed a chore. He not only had to climb up a steep and constant trail, but remain sure of foot. He did well, with just a little coaxing and a nudge or two from my heels. I could see and feel his body expending energy as the sweat and heat on his coat melted the snow falling upon his neck.

It was just after dark when we made it to the pass, and now we had no choice but to continue on. The exposure to the wind was unsettling, but it was a thunderbolt of lightning that gave us both a start.

There was no warning and when it struck a large tree on the edge of the pass, close by, we were startled by the spectacle. The flash and crack came from the heavens to split a big old fir plum down the middle. It lit a fire at the base that began to burn, slowly at first, crackling the old dry timber, to then ignite into a blazing torch as the flames got to the summer-dried needles. The hand of God had made its mark and done so as if with anger. If it was aimed at me, he'd missed his mark, but the message had not.

My duds, like the rest of my light provisions, now left me short. Frost bit at my fingers through the thin leather of my old work gloves, and where one finger on my right hand protruded, it was now turning numb. I had been foolish in leaving without proper preparation and was now paying for my disregard. Star sensed the difficulties ahead and I questioned the judgement of my decision. I had erred and we both needed to get off the mountain or we'd be frozen stiff in this early winter snap.

It was now as dark as ink, but with fortitude and luck we put the pass behind us. However, we were no further from trouble as we were travelling blind and Star was fearful. I had to push him on, when out of nowhere, I was walloped from my mount by a large fir branch that caught me on the forehead. I had not see it coming, but I felt the strike of the blow for just a second, then nothing.

# 6

## LOST

*Owl Creek Mountains, Wyoming*

When I awoke a thick layer of snow covered me,
with just the toes of my boots sticking out. It was
Star who had brought me back to life, licking the
ice from my face. I was to learn later that I had lain
in that snowdrift for the best part of eighteen hours
and survived. How I did so, I do not know. That
should have been my end, there and then, in a
silent peaceful sleep, but it wasn't to be. Had my
horse, my only friend, been my saviour? Or had I
been woken so that I might experience the misery

of a slow, freezing death? The devil knows no mercy.

I was in a poor state. Just getting to my feet was a major effort, and I had no strength to get back on my mount. I took the reins in frozen hands and walked Star down the slope, my legs and arms numb as wood from the cold. I was now well off the trail and hopelessly lost, but at least I was coming down off the mountain. My jacket was frozen stiff and ice was heavy on my moustache. Both of us now had no choice but to keep going in the faint hope of making shelter. In my heart, I held little hope as we pressed on.

After what seemed like a trial of endurance, it became dark and desperate. I was close to collapse and knew that we were now wandering aimlessly. It was just one laboured foot in front of the other, so when I walked into a near buried wire fence, I knew that the thin twisted wire with its barbs signalled our only chance. I was close to dead, but somehow we had stumbled on to a property. Somewhere there was a homestead, but where? Do I turn left or right along the fence? Was this the boundary of an upper or lower paddock? I guessed that the occupied land backed on to the mountain, and that this was as far as they had cleared. If I was right, then I would need to follow the fence down. But if I was wrong, then we would die. By now, both of us were on our last legs. Star gave me that look.

'Hell, I don't know, horse,' I mumbled from numb lips.

His instincts told him to keep going down, off the mountain, so he twisted his body side on to the fence and faced down the slope.

'Well, OK, we'll go down. But if we're wrong, don't blame me,' I croaked.

We followed the fence for nearly 300 yards then it stopped. My heart sank. There was no corner post or connecting fence, no slip rail, nothing. It just stopped. To turn around and head back up the fence line struck fear into my frozen brain. I had not only run out of strength, but also determination. I was spent. Then I saw it, the handle of a shovel protruding upright from the snow. I used all my strength to shuffle the ten or so paces to the implement. On examination, I could see that it was not weatherworn from years of neglect, but smooth from recent hands that had used its employment. To leave a tool like this on site would seem to indicate that I was not too far from habitat.

It was Star who heard the sound as my stiff collar was up over my ears. He lifted his head and snorted. It was an axe splitting wood. It sounded less than fifty yards away, but I could see nothing. I trudged on with stilted jarring steps through the snow and the chopping stopped. Had I imagined it? Then a young voice called in surprise just to my left.

'Ma, stranger!'

I went to call back but nothing came out, I was mute as if my jaw hinge had rusted tight. I slowly lifted my hands to show that I came in peace, but the owner of the voice had disappeared as if into a wall of white. Each footstep felt as if it was to be my last and I had trouble staying upright, even in the snowdrift that was above my knees.

My eyes were now barely open and my eyelashes heavy with ice. It was as if I was in a room of clouds. Everything was white, just totally white with no horizon, no shapes, no up, no down. I had heard the stories of being close to death, of conversations around the campfire from those who liked to tell stories, of seeing a light, a brightness, an expanse of white as they prepared for the crossing. I now wondered if this was true, and what I was experiencing was my departure from this earth. If it was to be so then it held no fear as I was beyond caring. I just wanted to rest, to have relief, to sleep the long sleep – that glorious long sleep of endless respite.

'Who are you with?'

It was a woman's voice as if on the wind, some distance away. It was a faint figure in a black skirt and a man's winter jacket, standing in the snow, with a shotgun in her hands and aimed at me.

I didn't care if she did shoot. I had run my tether. To lift my leg just one more step was beyond me. I felt Star nudge me in the back with his snout and I tried to move, but couldn't. He nudged again and I fell forwards into the snow, which enveloped me, but I had no feeling of the ice cold upon my face. For all of the sensation I felt, I could have fallen into a bail of cotton. I closed my eyes and let go. I was too tired to care. I just wanted to relax and rest, so that I could sleep, forever.

# 7

# WARMTH

*The Rowland Farm*

'Mamma, his eyes are open.'

I had no idea where I was but I felt at ease and comfortable, but not of this world, as if separated and distant. Then I saw the glow and smelt the oil burning from the lamp.

'You with anyone else, mister?' The voice was abrupt.

Was she talking to me?

'You with anyone else?'

She was talking to me. I peered through squinting eyes towards the light of the lamp that was now behind her head. The shape of her face filled my view but I could see no features.

'Water. You got water? Very thirsty,' my voice croaked like a frog.

'I'll get him water.'

'No, stay there, Josh. No water until we know who he is, and what he's doing here.'

'McDermott, I came through the pass. Thirsty.'

'On your own?'

'Yes, ma'am, just me and my horse.' My words were stilted and slow; my voice didn't sound like mine, and my throat was dry, as if caked with sand. I lifted my head and forced my eyes to stay open and the lamplight glowed like a halo behind her head. Her hair, pulled back, had small tuffs that had come loose and seemed to float in the warm light. 'Water.' My head dropped back on to the straw.

'Get the water.' Her words were sharp.

I closed my eyes and waited, but it seemed forever. Had I been abandoned?

'Lift your head,' came her command.

I felt a hand grip my shirt just below my chin and pull as I lifted my head. A ladle was put to my lips and never had water tasted so sweet. It ran over my cracked lips, into my dry mouth and across my swollen tongue. I felt it trickle from the sides of my mouth as I gulped. I drank on, quenching a thirst that could have only come from the fires of hell.

'We don't have much here, nothing to rob. We'll give you comfort and get you back on your feet, then you'll have to go. You can stop here in the barn. Josh will stay with you, a little, till settled. I'll be in the homestead with the door locked, and I have a gun.'

'My horse, Star?' I twisted to bring myself up on to an elbow, to prop.

'Here in the barn and in better shape than you, but you'll have to pay for feed.'

'I've got money.' I felt my tongue touch the burred and broken skin on my bottom lip.

'I know. We've emptied your pockets and your valise, and will lock away your guns. Nothing's been taken. Your jacket and boots are drying. You'll get them all back, but we need to be cautious.'

I guessed that the stash I had squirreled away in the coffee pot had not been found, only the travelling money I had kept in my jacket. 'I'm no threat to you, ma'am, or your family.' My jaw felt sore as I spoke. 'I'm just grateful that I found you and appreciate your hand of giving.'

I couldn't see her face clearly but her tone softened, a little, when she said, 'It is the Christian thing to do, but we have little and winter is now upon us early.'

'Yes, it sure is, ma'am.' I lifted my hand and touched my lip with a wooden finger. 'I expected a little snow over the pass, but the fury of the storm caught me short. You are indeed a saviour.'

'Caught us as well. And it was the hand of God that saved you. Had my son not been forced to go out for firewood, then you would have frozen to death in the yard without our knowing. I fear this will be a long, harsh winter, and we don't have much in storage.'

She had stressed again the poor state of her winter supplies, so my arrival was more than an inconvenience. I took note that I was an unwelcome visitor, but she and her boy had saved my hide and for that I was most grateful. I eased my arm out from my side and laid my head back on to the bed of straw. My body felt as heavy as lead, my feet like blocks of wood, and as I closed my eyes, I could feel a blanket being drawn up to my chin and hands tucking the quilt in under my body. It was as if I were a young child being tucked up in bed. I wanted to open my eyes and acknowledge my appreciation, but it was beyond my strength and I drifted into the serene comfort of deep sleep where cold, thirst and hunger abate their persecution.

# 8

# THIS IS US

*The Rowland Barn*

A slice of sunlight shot into the dark barn, reflecting off the snow outside and casting long shadows. It was pleasing to the eye, but held no warmth as the air remained cold to the skin. The boy eased the door open a little more as Star whinnied from his stall.

'I'm awake, boy, and of this earth,' I called. 'More or less.'

Star responded to my call then quietened.

'It's over. The storm is well and truly over. The sun's free of the cloud. Be setting soon though.'

Setting? Did he say, setting? I lifted my head. 'How long have I been sleeping, young man?'

'All night and all day, sir. You have not stirred. Ma said to just leave you be to wake in your own good time. She said I should tell her as soon as you do, though.'

'You've been here with me?'

'Yes, sir.'

I was impressed. 'You better go tell her.'

I could feel my bones creak as I lifted myself upright to sit. My head ached and my neck felt as if I'd been struck from behind. When I sat upright, the pain extended up to the top of my head. I sat still, not wanting to get up or to lie back down. I was stuck.

'Come on, let's go,' I said out loud and began to count. 'One. Two. Three,' then pushed myself to my feet with difficulty.

'You feeling right now?' came the woman's voice.

I turned slowly to face where the voice had come from but could see nothing. 'Fine and dandy, ma'am,' I lied.

'No need for you to get up.'

I could now see her outline. 'Oh yes there is, I

need to relieve myself, thank you.'

'My son will show you where.'

He responded quickly. 'Follow me, sir.'

'You'll have to do more than show me. I'm going to need to lean on you. I feel like my head is about to burst along with my bladder.'

The lad gripped the crook of my arm through the quilt as I tucked it into my side. His hands were firm and strong.

'Good strong grip, young man. How old are you?'

'Fourteen.'

'Name?'

'Joshua Adam.'

I started forwards in small stilted steps like an old man of eighty or more. 'Are you called Joshua Adam of a day or just when you are in trouble?'

'Just Josh.'

'Well pleased to meet you, Josh. I'm Gabe. The full handle is Gabriel Elijah.' I pushed my free hand out from under the blanket as I spoke, to steady myself on the barn wall as we walked. When we came to the corner of the barn I asked, 'How much further?'

'Up the back a way.'

I looked up and saw the snowdrift, which extended across to the little house.

'Are we out of view of your mother, Josh, cos I gotta go, quick.'

'Yes, sir.'

'Just let me prop against the wall and excuse my indiscretion if you would, but I'm going to disgrace myself if I don't go here and now.' My numb fingers fumbled with my belt, now in a race to free my spout. I was just in time and the relief was a pleasure all of its own.

When I stumbled back around the corner of the barn, I was greeted.

'That was quick.'

I looked up and got my first good look at the woman, and could see that she knew what had happened.

'Sorry, ma'am, the call of nature was too strong and I was feeling weak.'

She was surprisingly tall and slim. I had expected to see a stout woman as her hand had been strong when I felt it pull on my shirt. Her apron was blue and pinched in her narrow waist, and when she turned side on to walk back into the barn, I could see that she had the kit and caboodle of a city woman, which made her look out of place. This was a fashionable farm girl who still couldn't help but dress like one from the town.

'Can I thank you again, ma'am, for your generosity? I wish to pay and maybe buy a few supplies, then I'll be on my way.'

She turned. 'Any payment would be appreciated, Mr McDermott, but we can only spare you a little.'

I was now close to her, Josh still holding my arm. The three of us grouped together in the doorway of the barn. I wiped my hand on the front of my shirt and held it out in introduction. 'Gabe.'

She took it reluctantly. 'Hannah. Hannah Rowland,' she said slowly as I briefly shook her hand and at last felt some feelings come to my fingers. Her palm was warm but hard work had left its mark with the roughness of dry skin.

'And your husband, ma'am?'

There was silence. Josh let go of my arm and moved next to his mother.

I sensed the difficulty. 'Your husband, dead?'

She nodded.

'Long?'

'Eight months.'

'How?'

'Mule kick to the head,' it was said as a matter of fact. 'Here in the barn. He lost a lot of blood. We couldn't stop the bleeding. He was unconscious when Josh found him.'

It was as if she was reading the circumstances from a newspaper. It was with a detachment that seemed not to believe that it had really happened.

'And you've stayed on?' I asked.

'I had no choice, Mr McDermott. This is us. This is all we own in this world.'

'No other family?'

'None that will help.'

Her comment came with bitterness in her eyes.

'I found your liquor.'

I paused then said, 'I don't need that now.'

'I know, that's why I poured it out.'

Her comment brought surprise to my eyes. 'Oh,' I said, not knowing if I should explain that while I had no need for it now, I would have had later. But, she had done something that I didn't have the strength to do, so I said, 'I occasionally have a nip when cold,' and immediately sensed she knew it was a lie as an eyebrow arched ever so slightly over her right eye.

'If you would like to wash up you may join us for dinner. Just beans and pumpkin, no pork.'

It was an invitation that I had not expected and it was a pleasant surprise. 'Thank you,' I said. 'That is most obliging, and beans and pumpkin sound more than fine.'

She turned to go and I turned to walk back into the barn, unaided, when I stumbled over my two left feet and fell on my face.

# 9

# SALVATION

*The Rowland's Homestead*

The meal was eaten in silence with each of us taking our time to make the small portion last as long as possible. Josh and I wiped our plates clean with our thin slice of cornbread, while Hannah did the same, but with her back turned after she had collected the plates and taken them across to the stove bench.

'Thank you, ma'am, that is good cooking,' I called, then looked around the cabin. 'Could I get some water?'

'Josh,' came Hannah's call as her finger tucked

the last of the crumbs past her lips.

Josh brought the pail to the table and ladled the water into a tin cup. The salt in the meal had stung my lips and brought back my thirst.

'Mr McDermott, I'm just going to clean up, then would you like to join us for a reading? We can do it at the dinner table before you return to the barn. My son can read.'

If she had asked me to shell corn to contribute to my presence in her family, I would have understood and accepted the chore with a smile. But a midweek bible reading seemed odd to me and also to Josh, judging from the look on his face. Nevertheless she had extended the invitation for me to stay in the warmth of her home and done so with some cheeriness and a hint of pride.

'Not Sunday, Ma?' said Josh.

I caught his eye and shook my head to let it be as Hannah continued to stack the dishes ready for washing. Josh quickly glanced to check that his mother's back was still turned, then looked at me and shrugged.

I could only guess that the desire for a midweek bible reading was about keeping me in my place. But what was she frightened of? That I was going to jump her on the quiet and lift her skirt? Did she think the word of God would keep me chastened? Sure, she was an attractive woman, but that was of no interest to me in my state, or any state of late. I had last had that sort of relaxation back in a bathhouse in Joplin. Four dollars each it had cost me and Hiram for some look-see and some handiwork. It was the last of our money and we spent it on the ladies. Two young women smelling of lilac and with soft skin that was as white as milk. The one with Hiram got her money for sport as he was over and done with in a wink, but mine had to work hard and egg me on. In the end, I just gave up and both me and Hiram left dissatisfied, but for different reasons. We said nothing to each other, with only ourselves to blame. Ladies' men, we were not.

While I would have preferred any other reading, even a bedtime story for children, I was, however, grateful for the company and appreciated the hospitality that was being extended to me. I was not used to the experience of such genteel company. I was also aware of my good luck to escape a frozen death and had gratitude to this small and incomplete family. In fact, had it not been for Josh and his wood chopping chores, my body would now be lying out in the yard, frozen stiff, only to be found once the snow thawed.

So I called back, 'Yes, ma'am, your invitation to join you in a reading would be most kind, and I am obliged to you.'

'Is there anything in particular you would like to hear?' She was carrying the family bible to the table.

'No, ma'am. I'm sure all will be agreeable.'

'And good for the soul,' came the righteous reply as she opened the large book.

'That too.'

'Maybe Isaiah 12:3. Therefore with joy shall ye draw water out of the well of salvation.' Then her piercing blue eyes set on mine. 'Where do you draw your salvation from, Mr McDermott?'

I took the water cup from my lips. 'I don't rightfully know.' I paused. 'For some men, salvation may have passed. It is not something that I have had a mind to dwell upon.'

'The well of salvation is never dry. You just have to drink.'

I put the cup down. 'That may be easier said than done. I fear my well of salvation may be too deep from which to draw and drink.'

Josh looked back and forwards between his mother and me as we spoke, as if watching a ball being passed from hand to hand in a school yard.

'I will pray that the water rises, so that you may

drink long.'

'Thank you, ma'am, that is most kind of you.'

'Josh.'

I was relieved that Josh had now been called into the conversation. I caught the look of confusion on his face as he took up the bible and carefully placed it before him. He then gently pulled on the ribbon to open to a new page and started to read, but I did not listen. I thought of what might have been, had I taken up land and settled as a younger man. Would I have become a family man with a wife and son?

When Josh finished, I averted the conversation away from righteousness. 'Very nice, Josh, very nice indeed. You write as well?'

'Yes sir, and add and subtract.' It was said with pride and enthusiasm.

'Capital,' I looked across at his mother. 'You have taught him well.'

She was silent and cast her eyes to the floor, but a smile showed her pride.

'I came across the pass to look for land to settle,' I said, 'and I expect that I will have to go further north or maybe west, but do you know if there is land available around here?'

Josh said with excitement. 'There's Emerson's place.'

'Emerson's?' I asked.

'Pa said Emerson's land was good and it's for sale. Fronts on to the river, too.'

Josh's mother remained quiet. Josh took his cue and went quiet as well. I sensed that that the young man was being put in his place by silence.

'Time for me to go, ma'am,' I said. 'Although I find it difficult to leave such good company.' I lied with ease. Fatigue had caught me up, and my limbs ached. I just wanted to sleep.

'Josh, walk Mr McDermott to the barn and take this extra blanket. It will still be a cold night.'

I lent on Josh's shoulder as we walked through the track in the snow to the barn. The lamplight glowed on the boy's soft, youthful features. Fate had now thrown a man's work and responsibility upon his young shoulders, and I wondered how he and his mother would manage this first full winter season on their own.

'How long have you had this farm, Josh?'

'Eight years.'

'Before then?'

'Chicago.'

'Oh, you East folks?'

'I guess, but I don't remember too much. I do remember the journey out here.'

'Was that good?'

'Yes sir, mostly by train. I do like trains.'

'They certainly are an exciting convenience,' I said to mirror his enthusiasm. 'Now, the Emerson property. Where would that be from here?'

'Six, seven miles, depending, down on the new road. Easy to find. Just follow the river. It has a sign up. I can mark where on a page if you have one.'

When we got to the barn I extended my hand. 'Thank you, Josh.' He changed the lamp to his left hand, rubbed the palm on his trousers and shook my hand with the firmness of a man.

'You think you might settle around here?' he asked, not trying to hide his interest.

It had been sometime since anyone had shown any excitement in having me around, and I found myself responding with agreement by saying, 'I do hope so. The little I've seen shows it to be pleasant country, when not under snow.' I smiled. 'What do you say?'

'I hope so, too,' is all he said.

# 10

# WARM TOUCH

*Leaving the Rowland Property*

Josh had made me a map, written out in his neat hand, in my notebook, giving directions and distances to the Emerson place. His mother wrapped some cornbread, it too, neat as only a woman can.

'I wish to pay for my keep.' I stood with my hat in my hand.

She was ready for me. 'I worked it out to be ten dollars,' and handed me a small piece of paper with the details. Then added almost as an apology, 'Or thereabouts.'

I glanced down at the bill. It was excessive and she knew it, casting her gaze to the ground to avert from mine as I read out the amount.

Josh's eyes widened with wonder as he heard the sum, as he also reckoned it was beyond reason.

'That's not what I worked it out to be,' I said, firmly. Then before she could stutter a reply, I handed her twenty dollars that I had in my hand, hidden by my hat and ready to give to her. 'You have only charged for food and lodgings, not care and comfort. You have sold yourself short.'

It was twice the sum she had claimed. The extra money was more than clear profit, and could buy necessities that would make life less severe this winter.

Her eyes lifted and smiled with relief but she remained silent.

'You never know, we may see some more of each other.'

She clutched the money to her breast and said, 'I would like that, Mr McDermott.' Then seemed to regret having made such a quick pronouncement.

'So would I, Mrs Rowland. I remain in your debt.' I turned to Josh. 'This is for you.'

I pulled my pocket knife from my hat, where it had been resting for this moment.

Joshua looked at his mother to seek permission to take it.

She nodded.

'A handy tool, no matter what your trade or job,' I said. 'No toy of course. The blade is best steel and sharp. Keep it closed when not in use or being maintained.' I handed him the knife.

'It's heavy!'

'Solid brass frame and cedar handle. Has served me well these past ten years and has a lifetime ahead, if kept clean and oiled.'

Josh looked at the knife with pride and read out the letters cut neatly into the handle – *GMcD*.

'You may like to carve your initials on the other side.'

Josh lowered his head as he looked at the knife and I sensed that the gift was a point of some small embarrassment. Maybe he had never been rewarded with a kindness from a stranger. I touched his shoulder, briefly, then extended my hand to his mother in farewell. I felt her touch, warm, as we shook and I let the connection linger, as she did also. With awkwardness we finally let go, both tongue-tied. It was a clumsy yet gentle goodbye of gratitude and kindness that lifted my heart considerably.

When I rode out, back through the unfinished fence, the way I had arrived on foot, lost and desperate, I didn't look back. I wanted to do so with a sense of elation that I had never known before, but I didn't. Instead I held tight to the reins, my hand still warm from Hannah Rowland's touch, as I felt my heart skip several beats.

# 11

# EDEN

*The Emerson Property*

As I rode down the slope from the Rowlands' property towards the river, the snow falls were already becoming patchy. The icy residue was beginning to melt, and the narrow wagon track was acting as a gutter to drain the runoff down into the valley. To each side of the trail was virgin woodland of blackjack pines, big and old, their dark green needles quietly whistling in the light breeze. This was a serene place that had stood as it was for an eternity, undisturbed and as nature had fashioned it. It was beauty to the eye and was having a most settling effect upon me, as if I was seeing a new world for the first time.

From what I could now make out, the Rowland farm seemed to be on the edge of a large, natural clearing of open grassland that extended up to the high ground behind the homestead. However, down from the mountain, just beyond their front gate, it was all heavily wooded land. From the barn, I had presumed that the land had been cleared, but now I realised that to clear and extend the property any further would be beyond the physical efforts of a young boy and his mother. This limitation to cleared acreage would keep stock numbers low, providing not much more than a subsistence living, albeit one surrounded by the most pleasing of views. But I doubted if any farm in this immediate district would be very profitable until the land could be cleared, and a farmer's co-operative established to collectively market their produce.

The nearest town on this side of the pass was Preston, maybe a day away or even a little longer, so with few neighbours, Josh and his mother were a little isolated. Such a situation would suit me fine and deserved consideration. It could offer me an alternative to the original country that I had in mind, which was on the other side of Preston, maybe two or even three days the other side, so the Emerson property was now an intriguing prospect.

When Star and I came upon the river, the sun was flashing through the oaks and on to the folds of water that cascaded across flat grey stones. Fish skitted and jumped free for a second or two near the far bank, which showed that maybe it could be relied on for a meal. It was a scene so soothing to the eye that it needed to be appreciated, so I dismounted and walked Star along the flat, wide bank. Scene after scene delighted my eye as we headed up stream, following the lazy bends in the river. There seemed to be no end to its beauty and it helped to recuperate body and soul.

The track, which Josh had marked and called the new road, followed only a little way in from the river's edge. It was wide enough for horses in tandem, yet the sign of recent traffic was light. It was good and firm under foot, showing the odd stone on the surface and little erosion from flooding, so I concluded that it would not weather quickly from season to season. Overhead was an enclosed canopy of heavy foliage from large oak trees that let the light through in small flashes upon the road.

As Star and I walked further up this valley road,

the ground became softer underfoot. It was a fine, sandy soil surface that I couldn't help but try out. Star responded when I remounted and took off like a shot, taking me by surprise. The light and shadows flicked as we galloped, making it difficult at times for me to see. But before I slowed Star down, I let him have his head and egged him on as I yelled at the top of my voice, 'Yeeeeee haaaaaaaaa.' What someone would have made of it all I don't know, but I had forgotten how good it was to be alive in such a beautiful country. As I pulled up, I put my head down close to Star's neck and felt his coat against my cheek. This was a fine horse and I appreciated him as much as life. He had been with me now for over four years and we had travelled far. He had taken me across the pass to safety and now on to this handsome place. He was my trusted companion, and the only one who had never questioned the blemished character of his master. I was lucky to be in his company.

I nearly missed the Emerson place. It was set off from the road, tucked into the foliage and close to the river but elevated on a natural mound. The sign had it marked for sale with a stock agent in Preston. No price was mentioned, nor detail on the size or boundaries of the property, and the sign looked as if it had been painted by the amateur hand of the now absent owner. The empty homestead was dishevelled, but the roof looked good and it had a number of modern conveniences, including an indoor hand pump and zinc trough. For a family, it was small and lacked privacy with no internal wall or hooks from which to hang blankets, but for one person like myself, it was an indulgence of the first order and a place where I could settle and be content.

I wondered about the history of the property. While the fencing was at least twenty years old, the dwelling seemed not to be more than ten, judging from the mortar joints in the stonework of the fire-place. The plentiful supply of river rocks had allowed the builder to be extravagant in design, filling the whole wall of the room right up to the peak of the roof. It was an impressive and impregnable construction.

I guessed that Mr Emerson's departure had been a sad affair. Josh's mother had told me that morning, when pressed as to the circumstances for the sale, how he had built this home for a wife and family, only to have her taken from him through consumption. How long he had struggled on trying to bring up their four young daughters on his own,

I didn't ask as it seemed to be upsetting for Hannah. Maybe Josh and his mother should have joined forces with the Emerson clan and become one larger family. They could have kept both properties, while working one until such time as Josh was old enough to take on a wife. But no such liaison was hinted at and Mr Emerson and the children had gone back East, leaving the property to be sold on their behalf.

The barn was smaller than I would have preferred but it did have a cellar and like the homestead, it was a sturdy building with external walls lined in river stones. The narrow joints, as used in the fireplace, showed the same level of detailed workmanship. I tried to calculate what might be the asking price, but had no idea as to its true value. The surrounding cleared land was also natural like the Rowlands', extending back towards the lower slopes of mountain pines. No additional land seemed to be cleared. It too was little more than a subsistence lot, but like the Rowlands' property it was a fine looking one.

In two hours, I had seen enough to get a sense of anxiety take root. The sort of feeling you get when you set your head on something, but are uncertain about the chances of realising such a notion. If I took off now for Preston and was able to ride through some of the night, I could be on the agent's door to negotiate settlement by morning. If the asking price was beyond my means, then I could continue on with my original plan and look further north or the agent may have something else on offer. But in my heart, I doubted if I would ever see any place like this again. It was, at least for me, a Garden of Eden and I felt an urgency to seal the deal so that I could settle in this valley and put down roots. This awoke in me a new and rousing notion of anticipation.

As I rode at a walk back down the new road, I pondered why such a desire had not been awakened in me before now. Was it the experience of my near death when crossing the pass? If it was, why hadn't other close shaves in my life done the trick? I had spent a lifetime of shunning any possibility of settling, of being tied down to one place, yet now it was if it was all that I wished to do. It was as if a light had shone upon me, guiding me to what others already knew and cherished from an early age.

I had to stop myself from daydreaming as I proceeded down the valley, thinking of what needed to be done to the property, and how I could sit on my porch of an evening and look at the fish jumping in my section of the river. My preoccupation left me short to paying attention, and it was Star that saw and acknowledged the figure running up the road in bare feet and waving his arms wildly.

It was Josh.

# 12

# FLIGHT

*A Fast Ride*

I was at a loss as to what Josh was doing there on the road some six or seven miles from his property, on foot and running hard towards me. And why did he need to wave his arms about to attract my attention? I waved back to acknowledge that I had seen him, and he stopped 100 yards ahead, exhausted. With fists pressed to his knees he bent over and tried to catch his breath, gulping in air before he vomited upon the ground between his bare feet. I kicked Star forward in a gallop, then dismounted as soon as I got to him.

'Josh, what is it?'

He remained bent over and expelled again but this time it was little more than water. I patted him on the back, still curious to his antics. Josh lifted his head but couldn't speak as he sucked in quick breaths, his left hand now pressed against his side and his face showing his anguish.

'Got Mother—' he sucked in some more breaths before the words came scrambling out in frantic haste. 'They got Mother, in the homestead, locked the door. I got away, to get help.'

'Slow down, Josh. Who's got your mother?'

'The men looking for you.'

'The men looking for me? What men looking for me?'

'Three men. One called Billy, he is with Ma.'

'Billy?'

Josh's words continued to tumble out between short breaths. 'They arrived just after you left and were asking after you. Ma and me said nothing but they saw the initials on my pocket knife. They knew it was yours. Ma tried to get to the shotgun to order them off but it was no good. He said that they came over the pass and had a score to settle up. Something about a reward you got for double-crossing his

74

cousin.' Josh looked straight at me. 'Gabe, Gabe, you gotta help Ma.'

I stood as if frozen to the spot. It was Hiram's cousin, Billy – Billy Tate, a young, tempestuous man I had met on two occasions. On the first, I had taken an instant dislike to him and on the second, I had cemented that verdict. Hiram could be mean, especially when drunk, but he was predictable. Billy was spiteful and erratic even when sober. The wise would be wary of the character of such a man, and I was one. Like a rattlesnake, you were only safe from the venomous bite provided you knew where he was at all times and kept your distance. To trust Billy would be a fatal mistake and it mattered little if you were friend or foe.

The news of Billy's arrival with two companions now hit me like a thunderbolt. It was something I had considered to be just a far-off possibility. I had thought that I was safe through time and distance, but in an instant I now realised how foolish I had been. Travelling far and fast had not given the protection I had thought. All that time, Billy and his associates had been close behind, and now their endeavours clearly signalled their intentions; they were determined to settle up. I should have known that bad news travels fast and that Hiram's kin would learn of his departure at the end of a rope and come looking for me. But that they should get on to me so soon was a revelation.

Of all Hiram's cousins I doubted if it was really revenge that Billy wanted. It was probably more the money that he was after. Hoping to get to me before I had the chance to spend it all. Hiram was not close to Billy, he had said as much in disparaging terms on several occasions, but that held no weight now. This was about blood and blood money. Here was an opportunity to take my reward under the guise of provocation and retribution. Billy was that sort of man and he was armed and dangerous.

Who the other two with him might be, I had no idea and it didn't much matter. What did matter was that Billy now had numbers. One against three is not a good match at the best of times, and for me this was not my best of times. I no longer had any resolve to fight. Not now after Hiram's hanging. I was not just too old, too tired and too slow – I was also spent in spirit.

The only satisfactory solution I could see was for me to take flight and get away. To lose this trio would be easy, now that I knew I was being chased. My tracks to this point may have been clear to follow, but then I had no reason to cover them.

Now, if I went cross-country, or even went straight on to Preston to pick up provisions and two extra horses, I could travel non-stop for the next week and be well clear of the State. They would have no idea in what direction I had gone and winter would cover my tracks and test their determination to look for a needle in a haystack.

I put my hand on the boy's shoulder. 'Well, if you lay low, Josh, they'll move on and try to follow me. They have no quarrel with you or your mother, just me.'

Josh was still panting as he continued to press his hand to his side. 'They have Mother. Billy has, and I heard.'

'Heard what?' I asked trying hard to measure my words.

'What he was doing to her.'

At first, I had trouble trying to figure what he was saying as my head started to spin. In less than two minutes I had gone from the indulgence of day-dreams with a light heart to a boy's worse fears for his mother.

'What did you hear, Josh?'

The boy looked up. 'He, Billy, told us to get outside and he bolted the door from inside. I could hear what he was doing to Ma. The other two were standing outside the door, laughing and saying things. They said they wanted to be next.'

I got back on Star. I looked down the track and across the river towards Preston. I knew I could outrun them but would have to leave now. Maybe, if I stayed here I could ambush them, lie in wait and do it on my terms. But I didn't want to take a stand. I wanted to run. What Josh was asking me to do was to ride back up to the homestead and confront Billy and his compatriots face-to-face and that was now beyond my nerve. I felt scared. I had to escape and dug my heels into Star and he bucked to go, then stopped dead. Josh had grabbed the halter and was hanging on for grim death.

'I want to go back with you.'

He thought I was heading back to the farm, not to Preston.

'Let go, Josh.'

'No, take me back with you.'

'I'm not going back, Josh, I can't mend this now. I don't have the stomach for it anymore. I'd be no use anyway. Best I move on and leave you and your mother in peace.'

Josh's eyes narrowed into a look of cold contempt and I couldn't blame him, but I would not be dissuaded.

'Then give me your gun,' he called. It was an ultimatum from a boy who was fast becoming a man.

'Can't do that either, Josh. Need both of them myself.'

He tugged again on the halter and Star's head twisted down.

'Let go, Josh, I gotta go.'

He tugged once more, then let his hand fall from the strap. Star stepped past him, close, and just as he was almost clear, Josh lashed out with his hand and struck the rump. The back legs instinctively bent to a half squat for just a second as Star's hoofs dug into the sand. Then, instantly the gelding leaped forward into a gallop, kicking up a spray of dirt.

As I rode away from Josh, a feeling of shame descended in an instant. It was just like the one I had experienced by the gallows, only this time it was deeper; a more acute disgrace of what I had done. This was dishonour.

I turned my head slightly, but did not dare look back over my shoulder, keeping my gaze fixed ahead. But it was no good – I had to look back.

On the road was the lone figure of Josh, standing dead still, as he watched me run out on him. A young man who had come to me for help – help for his widowed mother who had accidentally got tangled up in my dirty business. Then out of the blue I felt like a soldier again, but one who had turned his back and run from the field of battle, abandoning a companion to be slaughtered by the enemy. I felt it in my stomach like an empty bottomless pit, a hollow that allowed the thumping of my heart to echo.

I pulled back on Star's reins and brought him to a halt and sat for a moment. Star pulled his head sideways to look at me, then turned side-on to look back at Josh. He whinnied. It was as if he was questioning my judgement, or was it my lack of character? I kicked my heels into him but he stood firm. I finally looked back with a lowered head.

'OK,' I mumbled softly, 'let's go back.'

When I returned and lifted Josh on to Star's back, neither of us made eye contact or said a word. My only glimpse, as he scrambled up, were of his feet covered with scratches and cuts that were now bleeding. As I dug my heels into Star, Josh wrapped his arms around my waist to hold on and pressed the side of his head against my back. I should have felt comfort from his hold that reflected his faith in me, but I didn't. When put to the test I had come up short. I was now making amends for my deficiency, but only after I had faltered so badly.

Star sensed the urgency of my demands and responded. Along the valley road, he opened up his stride as if in a picnic race on a grass track. His neck and head stretched out low as his hoofs thundered, while I bent forward with Josh clamped on to me.

We got to the corner where the track to Josh's farm met the new road, slowing only long enough to round the bend and begin the climb up into the foothills of the mountain. The road twisted and turned as we gained height, but the country was still open enough to ride fast. The exertion by Star, however, was high, as he was now galloping uphill at full tilt. The sweat on his neck glistened to show his immense effort.

By now, my head spun as to what I should do on arrival. There could never be any concessions with Billy, but the other two with him may listen to some horse sense, or so I hoped. They were not kin to Hiram so this was not their fight.

Five chambers of my pistol were loaded, but apart from a casual glance, it had not been checked or cleaned since I had come over the pass. That was housekeeping yet to be done. My handgun had been subject to ice and snow, then stored by Josh's ma and returned to me this very same morning. It was the same for my Springfield but that wasn't loaded, and the rifle cartridges were separated and stored in my travel wallet.

As the country now became closely wooded on each side of the track, my head told me that I should cut back into the forest. Soon we would be at the homestead and on open ground, and our approach easily seen. If we entered the woodlands I could stop and observe, plan and prepare, and then come forwards on my terms with my loaded rifle, to engage Hiram by either voice or fire. But if Josh was right, if Billy and his associates were having their way with his mother, then I had no choice but to act immediately.

Star galloped on up the slope towards the clearing and he was near to spent. The sweat on his neck was now streaking white as I urged him on with Josh repeating my words, 'Go, boy, go.' I took my right hand from the reins and passed it across my body and felt for my Army, its handle forward on my left hip. I needed a plan, a course of action to resolve the situation but I had none. It was now too late for that. I would have to let this unfold as it saw fit, and then respond. My late acceptance of Josh's plea had initiated the fight and haste was now the necessity.

We broke into the open with bright sunlight

causing me to squint. The homestead was now some hundred yards or more to my left front. Star galloped past the mounds of snow near the unfinished fence, his hoofs kicking up wet muddy clumps high into the air. Seventy yards out I saw the first figure, flashing up and down erratically in my jumping vision, dressed in dark clothing and now turning towards me with surprise, yet not making any motion to draw his weapon. Star raced on, his hoofs thumping to his unstoppable advance. The figure went to walk forwards, only then to realise that he may be run over, so he backed away to look up at what this magnificent horse was carrying – an old man and a boy. Yet, he must have sensed our determination and turned to warn the others of our approach.

I pulled Star to such an abrupt halt that he turned and twisted his head to the side to lessen my brace on the bit in his mouth. His rear hoofs skidded for a moment, sliding to a stop, then pranced to keep his balance on the wet and muddy ground. Josh released his arms from my waist and slid off the mount even before Star was stationary. I went to call to him but it was too late. He was down and running with bare feet, trousers cuffed just below the knee, racing towards the door of the homestead.

Just as Josh jumped up on to the small porch in a sprint, the door opened and two men emerged, the first groping for the weapon on his hip. It was Billy and Josh ran headlong into him. The impact forced Billy back on to the figure behind him, and all three seemed startled with the sudden clash and caught for an instant in confusion as to what was happening. Star continued to twist, taking my view away from the happenings, while I pulled desperately on the reins to turn him back. When he stopped, I was now facing away from the door, so I turned my head, straining to see and out of the corner of my eye, I saw Billy grab Josh around the neck while he pulled his handgun free from its holster.

Instinctively, I went for my gun just as the noise of his shot echoed into the valley and the power of a lead slug struck the back of my left shoulder. The force knocked me forward, as if I had stumbled in the saddle, and the surprise of this event was such that I called out, 'God, I'm hit.'

# 13

# EYE TO EYE

*For the Rest of Eternity*

I'd been shot and wounded on three previous occasions. Two of those times happened when I was wearing a uniform and bearing arms in battle, but they were not impressive wounds. The first shot went through the leg, high up, behind the back of the bone and close to the buttocks. It was a flesh wound and I was lucky. However, it frightened the life out of me. The ball hit with such a whack that I'd thought I'd been stung on the backside by a long, swift schoolmaster's cane. Hershel Gibbs, who

was beside me in the line as we advanced, heard my
'yelp' and saw me skip before he saw the blood on
the seat of my pants. We had joined up together,
Hershel and me, and he was a dependable companion and good company. He was also a man to
trust, so it was his wide-eyed expression that caused
me instant concern as I could not see the wound.

'You're shot,' were his words of surprise and affir-
mation.

I gripped at the back of my leg, then lifted my
hand and saw only a small blotch of blood upon my
palm.

'It's minor,' I said, not knowing what else to say.

But when I felt down to my crotch and between
my legs as we continued forwards, I touched a hole
on the inside trouser leg and felt a warm wet patch
of blood that was getting larger. Yet, surprisingly, I
felt no immediate pain, so continued with my
stride.

'You're as white as lace, Gabe,' said Hershel.

I kept stepping forward, but now my feet seemed
to stumble, and I felt a chill descend upon me as if
I had been taken from a warm drawing room and
thrown into the cold night air.

'He's hit,' called Hershel to our sergeant.

'Where?' responded one of the corporals from

the flank of our platoon.

I went to speak, but couldn't get a word out.

'The leg. Bleeding bad,' said Hershel as he now gripped at my sleeve to keep me upright.

'Fall out, McDermott,' came the command, followed by, 'Close up and fill the gap.'

I stopped and let the ranks of the platoon pass around me with their rifles held high and their faces grim as if not game to look. I dropped the butt of my rifle to the ground to support my weight from my shaking legs as I stood and watched them continue up the rise, across the corn stubble and into battle. Small puffs of smoke on the ridge could be clearly seen before sounds of fire met the ear. A man would fall, his body an obstacle to the following line of troops, which would open then close their ranks as they passed, continuing forwards and into the fire. I anxiously looked to where Hershel was in the line and where I had been. On and on they advanced, when, in a puff of white, he and twenty men fell in an instant to a shot from the Federal artillery. As the smoke cleared and I saw the sprawl of twisted bodies, I felt myself go numb. At that moment I wished that I had been with him. Beside Hershel Gibbs, my stout companion.

'Can you walk?' came the call from one of the

stretcher-bearers, an older man with a pipe clamped tight between his teeth as he pushed his trolley behind the advancing troops.

I nodded, unable to say a word.

'Then, son, best you make your way back to the station for treatment.' His words came from the side of a tight mouth.

I turned in a daze, to hobble back to where we had assembled for battle. The sound of thunder was now behind me, and I felt like a deserter when I arrived at the casualty station. The orderly sat me down, legs wide apart, and wrapped my thumb in gauze and made me stick it into the larger of the two holes in my leg. It stemmed the bleeding until a surgeon could inspect the wound, while I sat shivering, as cold as ice. Later, as the wounded started to arrive in numbers, I shifted my back to a tree, watched as men whimpered and asked that they be remembered to their mothers and wives before they passed. It was then and there that I was separated from my youth for the rest of eternity.

The second wound also occurred during an advance into battle. I was struck on my right foot by a Minie ball, which completely removed my little toe. It was the first shot of the engagement and signalled the start of the battle for our company. Once again I had no feeling of pain, just the sensation of a warm wet foot in my boot. This time, however, I was not going to fall out of the line. I pressed on believing then, as I do today, that I had been shot by mistake from within my own ranks. A discharge from a rifle by a nervous man to my far side who had lowered his muzzle to re-check that his rifle was loaded.

At the end of the battle, I saw the man who I suspected had caused this unintended wound. I was having my foot attended to at the casualty station and he was lying upon a broad timber railing. The lower part of his right leg was completely gone and he was humming the tune of Bonnie Blue Flag. He had been given an opium pill and when he saw me looking at him, he smiled. I smiled back. What good is blame? I was lucky to be alive, even if I could no longer count on ten toes.

The third gunshot wound came years later when I was overseeing a slapdash bunch of cowhands who had been hired at late notice to move eight hundred head of cattle to Baxter Springs. The truth was, Mr Allan had concerns that they may try and filch some of the head for themselves, so I'd been sent to keep an eye on them and to get the lead out of their backsides. They were being paid on a daily rate and were dragging this drive out for all it was worth.

I also had with me the government papers that cleared the stock of quarantine. I had put these into the inside right pocket of the heavy woollen jacket I was wearing. In that same pocket I also kept a small flask of brandy wine that was about half full. This drop had been recommended to me by the wife of a saloon owner to relieve the discomfort of a nagging sore tooth. As luck would later have it, this pocket was the precise spot where the shot struck.

The bullet went through the outer lining of the jacket, through the folded papers, and into the side of the brass flask before finally entering my chest. The bullet broke a rib bone and became lodged near the lung. It pushed me sideways, near out of the saddle, before I slumped forwards, desperately trying to catch my breath. I pushed myself upright and asked the obvious question through clenched teeth. 'Who was the son of a bitch who did that?'

'Me,' came an uncertain reply.

I looked down at the cowhands who were standing in a gaggle near the fire and saw Nigel, his weapon still drawn.

'You shot me,' I said, once again stating the obvious.

'I know,' he replied, while still pointing his revolver at me.

'Why?' I said, still trying to get my breath.

'Because I've just about had enough of you and your ways,' he said, but his voice now betrayed his conviction to get rid of me, and I saw that his hand was starting to shake.

I straightened up and felt the pain in my chest as if I'd just been branded by a red-hot iron. 'Well ain't that too bad,' I grimaced as I went for my gun.

I took my shot as a wounded man from the saddle and at a target surrounded by other men. It was to be one of my best. It struck him in the forehead, above the left eye, and he fell to the ground like a dropped sack of oats, causing the others to jump back out of the way with a start.

'Who's next?' I yelled. 'I've still got four more shots. Has anyone else had enough of me and my ways?'

They all shook their heads together like a chorus line of dancing girls.

It was that last wound that had given me the most trouble. I was older, much older, and it took a long time to heal, making it difficult for me to fully exert myself, especially when lifting. Just trying to get a saddle on a horse was a real affair. Getting it off, I would let it drop to the ground, guiding it to where it fell. The wound and the circumstances also sapped the trust I had in my own judgement. Nigel had taken me by surprise. I should have seen it coming but I didn't. And he should have killed me, but I was saved by some government papers and a brass brandy flask.

And now this was wound number four.

I tried to push myself upright, but it felt as if I was trying to extricate myself from a barrel of molasses. My arms were heavy, drained of strength, and unable to help. Just keeping my head upright was an effort. I pushed with both hands on Star's neck and he seemed to raise his head to help, but it was no good. I slumped forwards, my face hitting his mane as I felt my weight shift to one side. I was unable to keep my balance and started to slide to the right, slowly descending towards the ground as my left leg went back and lifted into the air then free from the stirrup. I looked down and saw the ground rushing up to meet me just before I landed head first, my right foot still caught in the stirrup.

'You got him, Bill, you've shot him dead,' came the call.

'Search him, I want that money. It belongs to me.'

That was the voice of Billy Tate, all right, and I felt a hand pull my foot free from the stirrup and let my leg drop to the ground, allowing my shoulders to roll flat. Star let out a snort and I could see his front legs in a blur as rough hands pulled at my pockets.

'Money. I got the money,' came the elated call.

'How much?' asked Billy in that weasel voice of his. 'Show me.'

I couldn't see but could hear the bank notes being shuffled.

'That's not enough. He got fifteen hundred. Not much more than a hundred here. Search the wallets and his roll.'

Star snorted again as the valises were opened and the contents emptied to the ground. I lay on my back looking to the heavens, trying to make sense of what was happening around me. I strained to move my hand towards my gun, but couldn't lift it from the ground.

'He's moaning.'

'Forget the old man, look for the money.'

The sound of a boot kicking the coffee pot rang out as the lid slapped shut, then open again.

'Hey, look, Billy.'

'What?' It was said as a cuss.

'We got the jackpot.'

'Let me see.'

I rolled my head to the left and saw the legs of the three figures on the other side of Star, close together with the coffee pot at their feet. They seemed to stand there forever, not moving, not talking. Then Billy said, 'Count it again.'

There was more silence and I closed my eyes, only to feel my head start to spin so I opened them again just as Billy said, 'That's five hundred there and that's five hundred there, so it's one thousand in all. And with the other hundred it's still missing four hundred, and I want it all.'

Billy's face appeared in my view as he leant over me. 'Where's the rest of the money, old man?'

I went to open my mouth, but nothing came.

'Are you gonna talk or just move your mouth like an old catfish?'

I moved my lips again, but nothing would come out.

Billy stood up as he continued to look down at me. 'You going to tell me, old man?'

I didn't even try to speak this time, even though I saw Billy step back then forwards to deliver a kick.

The toe of Billy's boot was aimed at my face, but he only managed to kick me in the shoulder on the first try. It was the second kick that made its mark, with the toe of his boot striking me on the bridge of the nose, and the blow hit like a hammer.

'Where's the money?'

'Got no more,' I croaked, but it was no more than a whisper.

'What did he say?'

'He said that there was no more money.' Josh's voice had come from behind me, elevated, forceful and clear.

'Come on, Billy, let's go. Let's take what we got and get out of here.'

'I'm not askin' any more, I'm telling. Where's the money?'

I tried again with all my might to reach for my gun, but I was in a nightmare where my mind failed to engage the body. I was in a dream of delirium and on the fringe of unconsciousness, which made me feel as if I was mired in some other place.

A bucket of cold water upon my face snapped me back from the brink as hands seized my arms and lifted me upright. Yet, I was unable to stand and sunk back down to my knees as a hand grabbed my hair and jerked my head back with force. I looked up and willed my eyes to focus on the blur that eventually took the shape of Billy Tate's face. He was agitated and angry, and I guessed he'd been drinking.

'I'm missin' four hundred dollars, old man. You is cheatin' me out of what's rightfully mine.' Billy let go of my head and started to pace back and forwards. I dropped my gaze and watched his boots as he took three or four steps at a time, before turning to take three or four steps back again. I looked up, and as he paced, he tossed an object into the air, then caught it in his palm. It was my pocket knife, the one I had given to Josh.

'Billy, let's go,' came the call from one of his associates.

Billy stopped and turned to me and grinned. He then walked over to Star and lifted my carbine from the leather scabbard. I heard the action on the rifle open then close.

'Empty!' he spat. 'Get me a cartridge.'

'On the ground. There's one on the ground,' came the reply.

Billy looked around then bent down and picked up one of the shiny brass cartridges that had spilt from my saddle valise. I was having trouble seeing but I heard the action of the rifle open and close to chamber the bullet. I forced my eyes wide just in time to see the looks of surprise on his two companions, as Billy pointed the barrel towards my face.

I remember wondering if Billy had the nerve to execute a man in cold blood. Shooting someone in the heat of battle is one thing, but doing it cold and calculating is altogether different. But he did seem to be liquored up with courage so I braced to meet my end. I guessed that he needed to demonstrate his ruthlessness to an audience, but why he was using my rifle was lost on me. His handgun would have sufficed. I was right before him, kneeling, and subject to any of his whims. He didn't even need to aim. I was close up and defenceless.

Billy lifted the butt to his shoulder with a smile, enjoying the moment and what he was about to do. Then, slowly and deliberately, he aimed, paused, released the catch and laughed, before slowly swinging the muzzle through a wide arch away from my face.

He stopped to sight on a new target.

I twisted my head to see what he was aiming at. I was confused as I followed the line from the barrel, before I saw that the muzzle was now directed at Star.

'No,' I called in desperation, but hardly a sound came from my mouth before the weapon bucked and cracked the silence.

The heavy lead bullet shot at lightning speed to thump into my horse, low on the front of his broad neck near the white markings that extended under to his belly. Star's nostrils flared from the wound as the air from his pierced lung exhausted and his dark eyes flashed white in fright.

He stood trembling for a moment from the mortal wound, then snorted and fell forward, legs bent but with his hind quarters still upright. He snorted again and this time blood flowed from his ruptured lung to flood from the nostrils on to the earth and pool around his snout.

I could clearly see the white star shape between the eyes of my beloved horse. It was the reason for his name that I had given to him as a young, frisky colt. Now his body twisted in pain like a stricken animal in a slaughterhouse. He shuddered then slowly rolled off balance, stumbling, to thump on to his side, legs kicking wildly into the air as he let out a sound, like a whimper. It was a final weak cry from such a strong, magnificent beast.

Billy looked down on me with a crazed grin. 'Guess you'll be walking now, eh?'

The loathing that overcame me at that moment was like a wave of heat from a desert wind. It rose in me through my body to build to a rage. He must have seen it in my eyes, because for just a second he seemed spooked. Had he been wise, right at that moment, he would have shot me dead there and then, because I vowed that I would get him while there was a breath in my body.

'What'd you do that for? That was a good horse.' It was one of Billy's companions questioning him. 'It don't make sense to shoot a good horse. And that looked like a good horse.'

Silence from the other associate gave credence to this view.

'Let's go,' said Billy.

'What about him? You going to leave him here like that?'

'Let's go, I said, if you want your pay.'

'You said you were going to kill him, not his horse.'

'I said, let's go,' yelled Billy.

'What if he comes after us?'

'He won't. He's nothing but an old man.' But Billy's words were less than convincing.

'He rode with Hiram and he has a reputation.'

'I'm not scared of him,' scoffed Billy.

The other of this trio just said, 'I'm going.'

I looked up. 'Go on, Billy, shoot me,' I said in a

voice soft and clear.

His eyes expanded and he licked his upper lip.

I knew that I had his measure. He had told his two companions that he was going to kill me but had balked. I was now offering him a second chance. 'Can you do it, Billy?' I said. 'Shoot a man when he is looking you in the eye?' My stare willed him to shoot.

Billy raised my rifle back to his shoulder.

'Go on,' I said, 'you can do it, but first you have to reload, so why not use your handgun, but don't close your eyes when you jerk on that trigger or you may miss. Just keep looking at me. Eye to eye.'

Billy's eyes shifted and he nervously licked his lip again.

'Eye to eye,' I repeated.

Billy hesitated. 'Shut up, old man, you hear? Just shut up.'

'Billy, do it and let's go.' The other two were now mounted and I could hear the hoofs of their horses turning and ready to depart.

'Eye to eye,' I said again.

Billy was now clearly agitated. His eyes darted from side to side and his tongue flicked his lips like a snake, while I kept my eyes fixed on his.

I gave a grin, only faint, and had to muster all my

strength to do it, but I needed to show that I had the upper hand – that I had his measure.

Billy lowered the rifle from his shoulder, slowly. Then with a startled grunt, he swung the butt with high speed towards my face.

The strike to my cheek came with a white hot flash before my eyes. It knocked me sideways to the ground causing the other side of my face to hit the dirt. I remained conscious but could see nothing. The sound of horses' hoofs thumped past me, and I expected to be trodden upon in their race to leave. And they were gone.

I tried to get up but was devoid of the necessary strength, so like a snake I slid on the ground towards my fallen horse. His head was lying flat upon the muddy ground and facing away from me, and when I reached him, I placed my head upon his neck. His dead body was still hot and wet with sweat from the fierce ride that had delivered Josh and me back to the homestead, and the blood from my face marked the white patch on the mane, as did my tears. Tears that had not passed my eyes in a lifetime, but that now flowed without regret as I cried like a baby, separated from its mother.

While I have always accepted the penalties for my actions, I expected them to weigh upon me and no one else. Star was my companion and my servant for whom I was responsible, and I had failed him as a friend and master. I had become poison to others around me, as well as the most pathetic of figures. Wounded in body and spirit, lying on my side with my legs drawn up to my chest and sobbing over a dead horse. It was all of my doing, but now there were others who were paying the price for my evil.

When I finally lifted my head from Star, I saw Josh. He stood looking down at me with dry eyes and a face set grim. From my position on the ground he looked taller, stronger and older. No longer like a fresh-faced kid or an immature juvenile, but a tough young man.

# 14

# SHAME

*Run Like a Rabbit*

Josh was silent to my grunts as he roughly assisted me to my feet. I hobbled into the homestead, unable to see from the left eye that had closed from the rifle blow. Once inside and as my right eye adjusted to the dim light, I saw Hannah, sitting, frozen, like a statue. She made no motion to recognize me, her gaze passing right through my being. Her arms were pressed to her chest, upright, hands gripping fists of her torn dress close to the neck. Josh put me on the bench so that I was able to prop my side up against the table.

I was bloodied from my wounds and needed help. Josh was able to provide it, but he did so with utility, showing no sense of care. A wad of cotton cloth was packed into the small entry wound on my back, close to my shoulder, and my arm was then placed into a makeshift sling. The bullet remained in my shoulder, which throbbed in time with the pain in my eye and head. The side of my face down to the neck was numb, and I now took the chance to feel gently around the collar bone, which I was sure had been broken, but surprisingly it registered no discomfort as I pressed and prodded along its length.

I called for water and my thirst seemed unquenchable. In the end Josh left the bucket near the bench and with difficulty, I could scoop up a drink into the tin cup. However, I spilt as much as I got to drink. Josh watched my wretched struggle but made no effort to provide any further help. Instead, he went over and sat next to his mother, close up and I watched as he let his head drop gently on to her shoulder. It was a pitiful sight, the three of us sitting in the fading light, all silent and broken.

If an invitation had arrived from the devil at that moment to dispatch me quickly to hell, then I would have accepted it with virtue. It was not that I just wanted relief from my wretched state; I could stand the hurt of my wounds as a penance. I just wanted to be removed from this place and the presence of Hannah and Josh. There had been little joy in their lives since the death of a husband and father, but any healing that comes with time and the routine of hard work had now been snuffed out and replaced with a new and deeper agony. I had allowed Hannah's person to be violated by vile men. I had allowed her last vestige of pride to be stripped from her. I had allowed her dignity to be destroyed. Josh had been witness to these terrible events that had now seen his mother retreat deep within and by doing so, I had separated Josh from his mother.

I sat in the dark with my humiliation of not being man enough to protect the innocent from the harm and violence that had followed me over the mountains. In a moment of desperate regret, I hung my head and prayed for forgiveness, but dared not take the name of the Lord.

As that night grew colder, I drifted in and out of fitful sleep and mulled over the prevailing circumstances time and time again. Josh had come to me for help, yet I had tried to run like a rabbit. When I did see sense and return it was with reluctance, and my response had been inadequate and my actions inept. I now saw myself as the harbinger of misery and felt the emptiness that comes with shame. I now wished that I had frozen to death in the snow.

Then there was Star. Over and over again, I recalled his death throes that then drifted into my dreams to wake me with a start. In the early hours, I lifted my head from the table and dragged my body upright, to stagger outside and relieve myself. I honestly thought that if I went to the barn I would see my horse. But he had not moved from where he had fallen outside the door of the homestead. Lying on his side in the cold, the roundness of his stomach protruding from the earth, a dark unmoving silhouette. 'Oh, my Star.'

After midnight and with no fire to provide warmth or light, the air was frozen inside that small farmhouse. But it was the cold in my soul that kept me awake. This longest of nights was a savage one that I will never forget. When sleep finally returned just before dawn to take me away, it came with no relief. My dreams were a fusion of the here and now and the past, intertwined in a cascade of faces that appeared out of the dark, some beckoned with a wave to then ask for an explanation of my long-ago actions. 'Why?' they would say. But I had no answers.

Then they began to turn their backs on me and join ranks, to group, standing, murmuring in discussion under the dim light of an overhead lantern. I pushed forwards, desperate to see what was now at the centre of their attention. In my dream, I could clearly smell and feel the damp wool of their coats as I forced my way through to finally see what it was that held their interest. It was a map upon a table that marked the Federal positions along with inked arrows showing the lines of advance. In an instant I could see that it was wrong and that the battle information was incorrect. I called out, desperately trying to force my hand to the table to point out the true positions of the enemy, but no one would listen.

'Can't you see? You will be killed. All of you will be killed if you advance on to that ground.'

But no matter how loud I shouted, I could make no impression. I had no credit with these men; they dismissed me without a glance as they shuffled from the table to take up their arms and check their equipment. I watched as they tugged at their tunics and adjusted their belt buckles, while holding their rifles upright between bended knees. I watched them assist each other, untwisting a strap across a broad back or smoothing a collar with a caring pat. A silent signal that it was done, fixed, a communiqué of solidarity.

I wanted to join them but they would have no part of it. I wanted to go with them, to join them in their folly, but they rejected me by exclusion and left me with just the diminishing sound of departing feet. Then they were gone. The door slamming shut behind them, and I was awake.

Hannah had refilled the bucket and dropped it to the floor. The edge had struck my foot and the noise had caught my ear. I awoke with a jolt and called out with a fierce grunt. Or had I startled her and caused her to drop the bucket? Her frightened breath sucked back before she shrieked out loud, waking Josh.

'Ma. Ma!' Josh's voice was of instant concern and he came to his mother with speed, and pressed himself to her side.

'Water,' I said to explain my outburst and the fright I had given her. As I moved my hand to the cup, I knocked it from the table and it fell upon the floor in a clatter. I went to move. Hannah took Josh's arm from her waist and stooped to pick it up, before filling it with water and placing it before me.

'Thank you,' I mumbled.

She did not speak to me, dismissing my gesture of appreciation. I drank, the cold water spilling from my lips. I was back from one hell and into another.

'Thank you,' I said again with gratitude.

Hannah remained silent. It was as if I was of no more consequence to her or her son than some household chore, like cleaning a plate or sweeping a floor. I wanted to explain but I had no explanation. I wanted forgiveness but I had made no confession. I wanted help but I had become a burden. What Hannah and Josh wanted from me was that I get out of their lives, and for that, I couldn't blame them.

# 15

## RETREAT

*The Road to Preston*

The opposite to love is not hate or loathing, or even animosity – it is indifference. Hannah hadn't spoken a word to me since I had ridden back into her life on a plea for help from her son. She now knew enough of my past to realize that evil had been travelling with me when she had offered me shelter and comfort. My uninvited intrusion had brought with it nothing but disaster, and now I needed to be got rid of, like a snake in the woodpile that had already struck once and might strike again.

But it was her silence that signalled her frame of mind. I was of little or no consequence anymore, just something that is best discarded without any further thought.

This I understood. If dwelled upon, my very presence would be a constant reminder of events. So, I was dismissed as no more than an observer in her household as she went about the daily routine, moving around me but not once acknowledging my existence. However, Hannah had plans and had spoken to her son and given instructions for my departure.

Josh led their big old horse, Bonnie, from the barn and stood her next to the fallen Star. Then began the task of removing my saddle, bedroll, valise, calico bags and harness from his cold carcass. I helped, as best I could with my good arm, but in the end did little more than watch and listen to the sound of stretching leather as the old horse pulled the rig free. Josh did not speak or seek any guidance from me during this task, so I remained mute as if struck dumb. But even if I had spoken, I got the distinct feeling that I would have been ignored.

Next, Josh pulled a rope under the rear quarters of Star, looped a lariat to the front of the rear legs and tied the running ends back on to the yoke harness on Bonnie. The grizzly task of dragging the carcass away from the homestead and down to the lower paddock began. My beloved horse was finally dumped without ceremony into a natural hollow in the ground, where Josh then shovelled the remaining snow from a nearby drift over the beautiful beast. Later, he would have to deal with the remains by the blade of an axe and a bonfire.

Bonnie was brought back up to the front of the homestead and readied for my leaving. When time to mount, Josh bent and cupped his hands to act as a stirrup to lift me into the saddle. I hesitated, not wanting to use him as a step, but I had no choice as it was beyond me to mount without his help. I dragged myself into the saddle and felt the familiar shape of the leather seat, but it was upon an unfamiliar mount with its wide girth and coarse coat.

Josh stood close by my leg as he adjusted the length of my stirrup, then checked the harness and flicked the reins towards me. His hand came close to mine but he did not touch or offer a farewell shake. He stepped back, signalling to me that it was time to go and I pulled back my heels, and the old girl ambled off at a walk.

I made no parting gesture nor did I utter a single word of thanks. This was no farewell but a retreat of the vanquished. For my silence I received the same. I had left them with an untidy mess of broken lives and a legacy of miserable memories. If, at that moment, I could have given my life to turn back the hands of time, so that I would never trespass upon Hannah and Josh's lives, then I would have done so gladly. If only life allowed all wrongs to be made right.

I rode on, sitting atop one of their few valuable possessions, their old horse, given so that it may speed my departure. But I guessed that they would have given the very shirts off their backs to see me ride out of their lives, forever.

My slow ride away from the homestead was under a dark sky with the possibility of rain or even snow. When I came to the fork in the road I didn't look to where it led to the Emerson place. That was now a lost dream. On the ground I could see the hoof prints of Star, where he had turned at a gallop to carry me and Josh to the homestead.

The trail to Preston now lay ahead, well-marked and easy going, but I'd be lucky to be there by the following morning at the slow plod of the old mare. However, I had no mind to go faster as it was uncertain as to what I would do when I got there. I had no provisions, no money for the purchase of goods and no future prospects. I could not afford a physician for my injuries or even accommodation, and I was in no fit position to continue on once I got there. But I plodded on like the slow turning wheel of a paddle steamer against a strong river current that drew it back towards the edge of a waterfall.

Caught in a world of my own thoughts and constantly chewing over my predicament, it was only when I was travelling up a small rise that I noticed the recent tracks of three horses. At a glance I knew it was Billy and his cohorts, and this thought seized me with fear. They had travelled this way after departing the Rowlands' place and were headed for Preston, while I had just assumed that they would have gone back over the mountain. The scuffed and kicked-up marks upon the muddy ground indicated that they had been travelling at speed, so I guessed that they were now well ahead of me. But where?

As I pondered what I would do, should I come face to face with them again, and about two miles further along the road to Preston, their tracks stopped. I pulled Bonnie up and searched the ground, which clearly showed where their horses had come to a halt and stood, then changed direction to cross over a clearing towards a stand of fir trees 100 yards away.

Had they stopped for the night? Why? The road was a good one and a horse could walk safely at night, even without a moon. I looked at the tree line as Bonnie began to plod on again towards Preston, while I became concerned that I would be set upon at any moment. But nothing moved except for the waving grass upon the clearing from the chilly wind.

Their deviation from the road was about 200 yards behind me when, blam! I was jolted in my saddle by the sound of a shot. It had come from within the trees and gave me a fright, letting an oath spill from my lips.

I supposed that the shot had come from a handgun and had remained within the trees, as there was no follow up crack through the air to signify that the bullet had been fired in my direction. Was it a shot for game by an unknown lone hunter? Or was it Billy?

Bonnie paid no heed and plodded on so I had to twist in the saddle to look back for any sign. When I turned my head forwards I felt exposed and just wanted to get away fast, but Bonnie felt no such apprehension and continued to trudge on at the same slow pace. Then, blam, blam, blam. Three quick shots, to be followed by another shot, then two more.

I stopped. Was it target practice or a shoot out? I stepped the old mare forward a few paces, but stopped her again as I was puzzled as to what it was I had just heard. I twisted in the saddle again, but could see nothing. If it was target shooting then there should be more shots, yet none followed. I waited and touched my hand to Bonnie to speak, as if to ask Star what he thought, then checked myself with embarrassment. I slowly turned the horse and faced back towards the trees, and without encouragement she began to walk in the new direction, and for reasons unknown I didn't stop her. Instead, I just let her tramp on towards the trees; towards the place from where the shots had come.

When we entered the firs, the wind turned icy with the shade and whistled through the overhead branches, while the mare's hoofs cracked upon the small twigs on the ground. I stopped and sat, looking, searching, but could see no signs of life. We stepped on a little further to prop again, watch and listen. Still nothing. I did this three times more and was ready to turn back when I caught a glimpse of a horse, unsaddled and untethered, standing off to the right. I pulled Bonnie up and observed, not game to move a muscle. The riderless horse saw us and quietly walked over in curiosity. I looked about, lifting in my saddle slowly and tilting my head to aid my hearing. But I saw and heard nothing, except for the wind in the trees. With my heart in my mouth, I let Bonnie begin to walk with the riderless horse now following on behind us and that was when I saw the first body, slumped near a tree.

# 16

# HELP ME

*Nest of Vipers*

The body was not that of Billy but one of his associates, half propped up against the trunk of a tree with his handgun at his feet. A wound to the face, just below the eye was clearly visible as the blood ran down his neck to cover his shirt and pool in his lap.

I eased myself up in the saddle again to look around and could feel the pounding of my heart in my chest. My sight was still restricted to one eye, so I turned my head for a better look. Was that another shape to my front? Another body? I edged

Bonnie forwards and was nearly upon it before I was certain. It was Billy's second companion. He was lying face down with his shirt pulled free from his trousers displaying where he had been shot low in the back, twice. His feet were bare with white soles facing me.

'Help me.'

The call caught me by surprise. It was Billy. I had ridden right by him. He was also sitting with his back to a tree, feet outstretched, his pistol still in his hand. I expected him to raise his handgun and ambush me, but then I saw the blood running from the cuff of his shirt and dripping from the hand that held his pistol.

'They were going to rob me,' he said, the words stilted as if he had just woken from a drunken sleep.

I slid from my mount and stood, slowly turning on the spot, surveying the ground around me. I caught the shape of the saddles, twenty yards or more away, up a slight rise and stacked close together. Behind it was a rope that had been strung between two trees over which a horse blanket had been draped. I walked over slowly, expecting to see who had attacked the trio but there were no assassins. The scattered dirty camp was all theirs, with bedrolls still upon the ground with strewn blankets and a pair of boots, neat and close together that stood upright and ready to put on. An empty whisky bottle lay on its side near the smouldering remains of the small fire, and a bent tin cup that had been stood upon was just off to one side.

I walked back to Billy, following the scuffmarks where someone had run in a great hurry, kicking up the pine needles from the ground to expose the dirt.

Billy hadn't moved.

'Thieves,' he said as I drew close.

I squatted in front of him and turned my head to look out of my good eye. He looked back at me as I slowly reached out and slid the handgun from his bloody grip. His palm fell open with the fingers splayed and still. I searched for the wound, which seemed to be a shot to the arm, so I pulled at his shirt sleeve and found the hole where the shot had entered. On further exploring, I found where it had made its exit and taken a chunk out of his side at upper chest height. These wounds required nursing but while they would cause discomfort, they were not immediately fatal.

'You'll live,' I said, 'but you will need to be plugged and watch out for blood poisoning.'

'I got money, I can pay you, get me to a doctor.'

I looked at him before I spat on the ground and reached across and felt each pocket of his jacket. In the two side pockets was my money, still folded, and in the top pocket I found the pocket knife I had given to Josh. I glanced down at my initials, then placed the knife in the top pocket of my jacket.

'These thieves didn't do a very good job stealing your money, Billy, and it looks like I've got it all now,' I said, in not much more than a whisper.

Billy said nothing, his face grey as ash as I finished counting the notes. It was all there, so I refolded it and put it inside my jacket. I spat again to stop the saliva that I could feel trickling from the corner of my still numb mouth, then stood and looked over at the two bodies before looking back at Billy. It was now evident that Billy had shot down his companions, one by surprise and one in the back as he tried to get to his gun that lay some distance away. But he'd been so inept in his ambush that one had been able to return fire from the flank, striking him on his arm that resulted in two flesh wounds. Who had fired that shot, I didn't know, but guessed it was the young one who was half-propped against the tree. The bootless one who was unarmed looked as if he had been shot down from behind.

I looked down on Billy's frightened figure. 'You're going to remember these two boys,' I said.

He looked up, confused.

'What?'

'You've never killed a man before, have you?' I could tell by the look on his face that I had read him right. 'That's why you couldn't kill me, eye-to-eye. You needed to be all liquored up, and do it from behind with surprise.'

'They were going to take my money.'

'And now I've got your money and you've got two companions for life.'

Billy looked at me with bewilderment in his eyes.

'These boys are going to stay in your head, Billy. They're the first and last men you have killed, and you always remember the first and last. It's the ones in between that get lost. At least for a while.'

Billy continued to look at me, befuddled.

'Help, I need help.'

'Don't we all,' I said, but the words were empty of emotion as I had no compassion in my heart, and luckily for Billy, nor anger in my head. I remember asking myself how he could possibly expect mercy from me? But here he was, now asking and expecting it in return. In truth, this was Billy's real character. His body was that of a man but his thinking was that of a juvenile. He had never grown into a man and in essence that's what made him so dangerous. His had been a life where he accepted no account for his actions, but they were finally catching up with him now.

I roughly pulled his shirt from his britches and with difficulty, ripped a strip of cloth from the tail with my good hand to plug his wounds. I then took the sling from my arm and used it on Billy. He accepted the care like a child being dressed, and as I pulled his good arm across his body, I told him to grip his elbow in support, then I bound the two together. This arrangement supported the wounded arm, but that was not my aim. He was now unable to use his arms and in particular his good hand. I then secured the wrist of his good arm to his trouser belt. He accepted what I was doing without protestation, and as if this was normal treatment for an injured man, while I was fully aware of the necessity to hogtie Billy. Like a snake, he may be lying cold now, but given time he would strike again.

It was beyond me to get Billy's horse saddled, and getting both of us on to the back of the big mare was also an impossible task, so we started walking away from the killing ground and the whistling wind, and over the open ground back to the road.

123

Billy moved with difficulty and made soft, whim-
pering sounds. His breathing was laboured which
meant that he may have broken a rib or two, but no
blood spilt from his lips so his lungs were fine.
When we got to the track, I pointed to a large, old
fallen pine and led the horse up to the trunk at the
lowest point and stepped up. I helped Billy follow as
I led him along the dry tree trunk, and walked the
horse until the saddle was at the height of my waist.
I then slid on and called to Billy to get on behind
me. I felt him shuffle on to the rump, then slump
against my back as I pulled the holster with my
Army Colt forward on my belt, so that it now sat
between my legs. I then turned the horse back to
the way we had both come – back to the Rowlands'
property.

It took Billy a while to figure where we were
going, but eventually he did. 'What you doing? This
is the wrong way to the doctor in Preston.'

'Not going to a doctor and not going to Preston,
you're in no shape, you need to get under cover
and get cleaned up.'

I'd lied. I should have gone on to Preston, but
not with Billy. I should have taken the money and
the horses and left him for dead. Without assistance
and on foot, it would take a most resourceful man

to make it to help. Of course, if I'd been ruthlessly wise, like I once was, I would have shot him dead, just in case he did stage a miraculous escape. But I was being drawn back to Hannah and Josh with a will that was not all mine.

'You're taking me back to that woman and her boy.'

I didn't answer but just let Bonnie plod on.

'I don't want to go back there.' He sounded like a spoilt child making a demand.

I sat in silence and listened to the slow and rhythmical clomp, clomp, clomp, taking us both back to Hannah and Josh. Billy slumped against my back, and I could hear him sucking in short breaths as we rode on with the sun approaching the mountain peaks to cast long shadows across our path.

'Sure am thirsty,' he mumbled.

'One of the reasons we need to go back. I'm out of water.'

I had lied again. All I could think about was going back, but what was I going to do when I turned up with Billy? For that I had no real reckoning. What he had done was beyond justification or apology. He would not be welcomed and neither would I, but somehow I knew that I had to return. I didn't know or understand why and can only guess that I was desperately seeking redemption, but in doing so I was going to bring back the serpent that had inflicted the pain. And in my simple state I thought that serpent was Billy alone. How foolish, Billy and me were from the same nest of vipers. Had you seen us slithering across your path, you could not have told us apart. Our natures were one in the same, maybe not in years, but certainly in character.

# 17

# RETURN

*Nowhere to Go*

Bonnie plodded back up the hill towards the Rowlands' farm with no urgency. She had no need to show any eagerness at the prospect of returning to home. This was just one more chore and tomorrow there would be another.

The two of us sat on board her broad back, riding in silence. I had no idea what Billy was thinking but my mind was filled with demon thoughts of what had been and what might be. The sun had now crossed behind the tall mountain peaks of the pass to cast long cold shadows, and I lifted my collar with my good hand then rested it back atop my Army. Billy didn't move, the weight of his head against my back.

I pondered on what I should do on arrival at the Rowlands'. My mind ran over the scene of seeing Hannah and Josh, and of them seeing me. In my confused state, I even considered the foolish possibility that I might be met as a returning hero, who had avenged the evil acts that had been laid upon them and was now delivering the perpetrator as a sacrificial gift. Fortunately, what little good sense I had, quickly told me that this was all delusion. I was bringing back no prize and nor had I been heroic. Fortune had played an unseen hand and delivered Billy to me, wounded and spent. It had also filled my pockets back up with my wages of sin. Under different circumstances, as a younger man, I could have used such a situation to my advantage, twisting the story to enhance my standing and reputation. But it was different, now. All pretence had gone from my life. Yet here I was, for some inexplicable reason skulking back to Hannah and Josh like a dog seeking forgiveness from the hand it had bitten.

Had I left them that day declaring my intentions to right a wrong, to chase Billy and his compatriots down and bring them to justice, or even gained new wounds from some daring action, then I may have expected some small approval, but none of that had happened. In fact, I was on the mend and could even feel the fresh chill of the wind against my once numb cheek; and since I'd taken my arm from the sling, I had felt no further discomfort other than a dull, constant throb. I was no returning warrior, just a broken old man with no future and nowhere to go. So what had convinced me that what I was doing was right? Even now, when I look back on these events, I shy with embarrassment at my rash audacity.

As we crossed the new road that led to the Emerson place, I stole a glance up the track, only to see Star's deep hoof prints where he had sprinted at full pelt the day before. But these marks upon the ground now seemed distant and detached as if a sign from long ago and from a different time and place – maybe a dream. We were now within twenty minutes of arrival at the Rowlands' farm and I was becoming apprehensive, yet I did nothing to address these concerns, but sat tight as if Bonnie was in command of my journey and not me.

When we came upon the fence, the light was becoming dim and the house seemed deserted as no lamp shone from the small front window. I cast a glance to where Star lay buried in the snowdrift, then towards what seemed to be a deserted homestead. The horse plodded on, turning its head towards the barn. I pulled her up short, just in front of the small home.

I sat, Billy pressed against my back, looking at the door as my mind raced as to what I would do and say. I had become frozen. I had no plan, not even an excuse for my arrival, other than the thought that I had nowhere to go. I was like a knight of old before the drawbridge, on the wrong side of the moat, seeking entry to the court but knowing that the news I carried would be treated with scorn.

It was Josh's voice from the side that caught me from my thoughts.

'Gabe, what have you done?' It was said quietly and not as a question but more as an accusation.

I turned to see the young man standing with the shotgun in his hands and held across his chest, as if ready to go hunting.

'I, I've brought back Billy Tate,' I said.

'The others?'

'Dead.'

'You killed them?'

Oh how I wished I could have said, yes. I sucked

in a quick breath. 'No, Billy did.'

'Why didn't you kill him?'

I had no answer and fell silent, before I lamely said, 'He's wounded.'

'Good. Now get him down, so I can kill him.' Josh's voice was calm.

I slid off the horse and turned towards Josh. In the fading light, he now seemed taller and heavier as he stood upright and armed. His eyes showed the fire of his anger and desire for revenge, and I was surprised. It was as if a year or two had passed and he had grown up.

Had it been Hannah calling for vengeance with Josh feeling obligated to follow, then that would have made sense, but this was her fourteen-year-old son who was not only calling for the ultimate punishment – execution, but desiring to carry it out.

My head was empty of words to reply, when from slightly behind me and to my left, I heard the door of the homestead open. I wanted to turn my head and look but couldn't.

'Why did you bring him back?' called Hannah as she appeared from the dim light to walk over and stand just behind Josh. Her face was set hard and she too looked older.

'He's wounded,' I repeated. 'He needs treatment.'

'But why here?' Her voice was cold.

I was still lost for words. I didn't know what to say. I went to speak and stumbled, 'I, I—' My gaze dropped to the ground. 'I had nowhere else to go.'

'Well, what makes you think you'd be welcome here?' Josh's words were spat at me. He then strode forward and for a moment I thought he was reaching to take the horse, who snorted as he approached, but he was reaching for Billy. He grabbed at his leg and gripped a fist-full of trouser that he jerked with all his might, pulling Billy to the ground like a bag of rags that fell with a dull thud and pathetic whimper.

He lay on his side and drew his knees to his chest and called for water. 'Thirsty.'

The request was met with a boot from Josh, striking the chest to expel the air from Billy's lungs with a rush.

'Get up,' said Josh with authority, 'get up, you dog.'

Billy sucked in, taking small sharp breaths.

Hannah remained still as Josh pulled Billy up by the hair until he was on his knees. He then stepped back and aimed the twin barrels of the shotgun at Billy's head.

'Water,' came the feeble request.

Josh seemed infuriated by the demand and kicked Billy again. This time the blow came to the stomach, below his folded and tied arms, and the kneeling body buckled forward. Josh stepped back and took up the shooting stance once again with the butt to the shoulder and ready to fire.

I wanted to speak, but what to say? I slid my tongue across my cracked lips to moisten them and held my breath, ready to hear that fatal shot and witness an execution by a fourteen-year-old boy.

# 18

# KILLING

*War*

The first man I killed was a youth just like myself. We met briefly on the field of battle. Two callow soldiers amongst many, caught up in events that overwhelmed our innocent senses. But we had no excuses. We had surrendered our bodies and souls, each of us, to our respective causes. This was our duty or so we thought. That we had not yet experienced the burn of hard liquor upon our tongues or even the sweet touch of a romantic kiss upon our lips was testament to our unworldliness. Yet, here we were, trained to kill with rifle in hand and bayonet fixed.

The day was warm, verging on hot, with sweat running down from my cap and forehead to sting my eyes. The smoke and dust obscured my view and I was out of breath and parched. My legs felt weak and my feet like lumps of lead as I was jolted from side-to-side glancing off other shoulders. But on we lurched towards a distant fence that marked the enemy line. The pace of our formation was brisk and getting faster, and I found myself having to run every now and then just to keep up.

Small flashes and little puffs of smoke signalled that volleys were being fired in our direction, to then be followed by the kick of dirt well to our front where each round fell short. But on we continued with our advance until we could hear the lead balls zing over our heads, or thump into the ground to skip and scoot into our ranks. Yet, undeterred we pressed on, each man fearful that he would be the one to falter, until we finally entered into the precise range of the Federal muskets where the fire began to take its ruinous toll.

Men began to fall.

Older, bigger men – men of purpose who had treated me as an equal – men whose company I felt privileged to share. Each selected at random, regardless of age, experience or disposition, began to drop to the ground suddenly, as if tripped by an unseen obstruction.

With each frantic step, I expected to be hit by the thud of a musket ball and prayed that it would be a swift and fatal wound with little pain. I could hear myself talking out loud, repeating our final instructions, 'Keep the line, keep the line, step up and keep the line.'

I looked straight ahead as my vision seemed to narrow. It was as if I was looking down the wrong end of a telescope. Someone shouted, 'Keep the line.' I repeated it out loud in response as if at prayers, 'Keep the line, keep the line,' I called, gripping my rifle hard with fear.

A man fell to my front, two ranks ahead, and I stepped over his body as our line came to him. I glanced down just for a second, a fleeting look, and saw his face. I knew him. I had seen him that very morning as we were forming up and he had nodded in recognition. He was a tall man with large hands. A farmer accustomed to the hardships of the land, who now lay upon the earth bleeding from a wound to the side of his head.

'Keep the line,' I told myself aloud. 'Keep the line.'

'Let's go,' came the yell from the front and we all broke into a shuffling run to the clink of buckles and the scuff of feet. 'Keep the line, catch up,' I called to egg myself on.

'Fill the gap,' came a cry from the front. A short man ran past me, a Scot from Texas, sprinting forward. He was much older and had a family; I had seen the locket that his wife had given him with the image of his two children. I ran after him, compelled to follow and help him fill the line. When I finally caught up to his side, I looked over towards him, nearly bumping against his shoulder as we ran forwards. He glanced back with a faint grin and I did my best to grin back.

Thirty yards ahead, the first line of our company were now at the stone wall where the Federals had made their holding line. We followed after them, ready for our turn. Now only twenty yards away, then ten, then five.

'Good God, a Federal,' I heard myself say aloud.

His blue uniform clearly before me as he stood up and aimed his weapon at me, eyes open wide above the sights of his rifle. I was now upon him, face-to-face, a youthful face, about my age, but there was no shot, he just looked. I lunged with my rifle, now only a pace or two away and with my bayonet perilously close to his chest. I pulled the trigger and felt my rifle kick, and in the haze of blue smoke he disappeared, as if swallowed into the ground behind the stone fence. Where did he go?

'Over first, laddie.' It was the Scot pushing me. I lifted my heavy legs, clipping my knee on the top of the wall before I fell forwards, dropping my rifle and putting my hand out as I fell towards the ground to land upon a bundle. It was the youth I had shot.

'Get up and help me,' called Jock, almost out of breath as he struggled to climb the fence. I turned and faced him and with both hands pulled on his jacket. It took all my might as I hoisted him up, his legs scrambling until over he came to fall on top of me, just as a musket ball thumped into the stonewall where I had been standing.

I scrambled to retrieve my rifle and get to my feet. The Scot was up and on his way and I had to run to catch up through the smoke and dust and crumpled bodies. Our platoon was now just a loose formation of scattered groups that chased after the tattered blue line of Federals. They were in retreat, pulling back over the crest and down towards the river and into the woods. We wanted to run on but were halted by one of the lead officers of our brigade who positioned us to face down that slope. The Scot questioned why we had not continued the pursuit, and had he run on then I would have followed, but the officer had called us to a halt to consolidate our position. We yelled to the left and right that we had seized our objective.

Then the officer called. 'Prepare for counter attack.'

'Load up,' said Jock and I followed his instructions.

The officer passed by us, close, with his sword in hand. 'How are we then?' he asked.

'Jim Dandy,' said Jock.

I said nothing, being busy with my musket.

'The lad?' he asked Jock, referring to me.

'Finer than Jim Dandy. He was across the wall before me. He's a fighting man.'

'Well done,' was all that the officer said as he moved on, but it was more than enough praise. My greatest test of not letting down my brother soldiers had been passed and recognised. My fear of failing diminished, to be replaced with a self-confidence that made me feel tall and proud.

Jock pulled the ramrod from his barrel and looked at me and grinned. I smiled back. I was in the company of men and being treated as an equal.

Had we been ordered into the woods, just me and Jock, to follow up the Feds, then I would have gone. I was willing to take all necessary risks to remain a valued member of my regiment.

I still remember Jock's face clearly to this very day. I soldiered with him, side-by-side, for the next year until his death. A death that did not come from shot or shell, but a fall from a horse, upon his head, while helping the artillery. It didn't even take place in battle but in winter as we sat tight and prepared for the summer campaign. He had offered to help, to unhitch their horses and take them down to the river. I wasn't there but I heard the news that same day. I should have felt something, some weight in my heart, but I felt nothing. No sadness, no remorse, no tears – nothing. I just kept remembering his face with that grin, and that of the youth I killed at the stone fence when I was with Jock. A face I'd seen for no more than a handful of seconds, yet it remained clear in my memory, and now it was grinning at me while I remained expressionless and numb.

# 19

# REDEMPTION

*Edge of the Abyss*

If I were to let Josh have his way, to let him squeeze those two triggers of his shotgun in an instant pique of retribution, then I knew there would be no going back. Yet, that rush of blood, that impulse to kill, to feel the satisfaction of self-righteousness, to fix a wrong, could be seen clearly in his eyes.

But killing fixes nothing. Life just doesn't work that way.

The explosive blast of either barrel would take off most of Billy's face, blowing his head back like a rag doll, to leave his body quivering, his fingers twitching and his legs jerking.

But then what?

Would the gurgling, croaking sounds from that bloody hole that was once his mouth beg for forgiveness? Would a final cry from deep down in the throat, a last call from within – the rattle of death, be one of remorse?

And what of Billy?

Would his departing soul be put to the ultimate judgement and damnation? And if that were to be so, then should not that same judgement be served upon Josh?

He was just a finger flick away from joining me in hell, but I knew that's not how he saw it.

Should I intervene? Was it my duty to do so? I was not the boy's father. And where were the protestations from his mother for the act he was now contemplating? I had killed men on the silence of others, so what right did I now have to interfere? Yet, as I looked at Josh, a mute prayer crossed my still lips. Stop this now, it said. Don't let this be. This is no way for a youth to lose his innocence.

I desperately needed an alternative, but what? I needed to dissuade Josh from his thoughts of reprisal, and I needed it now. I needed time. But no answer came to my call. The Almighty, whom I had dismissed with scorn for a lifetime, chose not to respond. I was to receive no hallelujah from on high and nor did I deserve one. If Josh was to be pulled back from the edge of an abyss, then I had to intervene on my own, and by doing so this act may also be my last shot at self-redemption.

I could feel Satan's hot breath upon my neck and hear the shackles of his harness jingle with anticipation. My feeble mind now spun like a top as I tried to find a way.

In desperation, I caught Josh's eye then said, slowly, 'If you shoot, Josh, then it will be over for Billy in an instant.'

'Good,' he said loud and strong.

'He'll be dead,' I said, measuring my words with the weight of consequence.

'Good,' he said again.

'But he will also be removed from the pain and remorse of this world.'

Josh was silent.

I kept my eyes locked on his, then continued, quietly and slowly. 'But does he deserve such mercy? Isn't a quick death too good for him?'

'Yes, it is.' Josh was forthright with determination as he pulled the butt of the shotgun tighter into his shoulder, showing he was ready to fire.

'Well, then, why not let him suffer first? Let him experience some of the pain he has endured upon your mother?'

Josh was silent but I could almost follow his thoughts as his brow creased. He coughed a barely audible sound from his throat before he spoke. 'What do you mean?'

My hand reached unhurriedly to my jacket and I pulled the pocket knife from the top pocket, and with one hand I eased it open. The oiled steel blade with its razor sharp edge flicked into place and extended from my hand.

'We could have some fun.'

'What fun?' His eyes darted just slightly from Billy to me then back to Billy.

'Cutting fun,' I said, holding the knife up to let the last of the evening light shine upon its silver blade.

'What cutting fun?' There was a touch of confusion in his voice.

I leant over towards Billy and gripped the hair on the back of his head with my free hand and pulled it back with a jerk. Then with my other hand, I placed the blade of the knife to his cheek and drew the needlepoint edge down the side of his face

144

slowly. A thin line opened on his flesh to be followed by a rush of blood that flooded from the cut. Billy sucked in a frightened breath and tried to pull his head away, but I willed my injured arm to hold its grip.

'Your turn,' I said, keeping my voice soft. 'You do the other side.'

Josh made a little sound so I stole a quick glance to his face and it now showed his bewilderment, but what I wanted to see was concern. I continued. 'Or, maybe his nose? This blade could cut his nose clean off. Ever seen a man with his nose cut off, Josh? Sure does look funny. Or ears? Now, there's a better start. One each. Do you want to go first?'

Josh made that little sound again, as if to clear his throat before talking, but he said nothing.

I seized Billy's ear and he tried to pull away, but I held fast as he squealed like a pig in a high-toned sound of anguish, of being trapped. I slid the razor edge of the knife over the top of the ear where it joined the side of his head. Billy's squeal became louder and the pitch rose higher. The blood flowed down his neck as the ear started to separate from the bone. I moved my body and lifted my arm so Josh could see clearly. I continued to cut. 'Coming clean off,' I said out loud as if carving turkey meat from the bone. 'You're going to like this knife, Josh, it's a good 'un.'

'Stop,' came the shout from Josh.

I pretended not to hear, but was not game to lift the blade from the ear should my false intentions be found out, so I kept the knife moving as the gristle gave way to the steel edge and Billy continued to scream.

'Stop it, I said.' Josh's voice was loud and clear with a mix of command and appeal.

I didn't look up as I spoke. 'What was that, Josh?' I said deliberately.

I felt his hand grab and grip my shoulder and shake. 'I said stop.'

'Why?' I questioned.

'It shouldn't be done.'

I kept my voice calm. 'What shouldn't be done?'

'Doing that. Mutilating him.'

'Why not?'

Josh's mouth opened, but no explanation came out. So I spoke. 'Is it OK to kill but not to injure? OK to blow his face to kingdom come, but not to remove an ear first? To cut him up a little, to cause a little grief and pain?'

Josh's mouth continued to open and close ever so slightly. Then he said it. He finally said it. 'No. No, it's not right.'

I saw Hannah move in silence to the side of her son. She pressed herself close as Josh lowered the gun from his shoulder, slowly, and with it fell the reins from Satan's grip.

I let go of Billy's ear and he fell to the ground on his side with his arms still bound around his waist and his knees drawn up to his chest. It was a pathetic figure that sobbed and blubbered uncontrollably like a hysterical child.

'Get up, you wretch,' I said and kicked him in his side.

'No, leave him be,' said Hannah. 'His maker knows what he has done and will hold a mirror to his soul. He will see and carry a stain.'

'Then what do you want me to do with him, ma'am?' I asked.

'I don't want you to do anything with him. He is of no consequence to this family, anymore. I do not offer him forgiveness, but nor do I offer him malice. He is of no significance. He is one of the disaffected.'

Hannah's judgement was spoken in a soft voice without emotion, yet the words cut the now cold evening air as if Billy had just been cast out of home and shelter by a curse. He lay on the ground and continued to sob uncontrollably as the words fell upon him. It was a response like that of an anguished child being scolded by his mother.

I looked at Josh, his arm around his mother, the other gripping the shotgun. Our eyes met, Josh, Hannah and mine. Then all three of us looked back down at Billy as if he was some curiosity, like an unfamiliar animal from another world.

# 20

# EXODUS - FINAL JUDGEMENT

*Dusk*

That night was my road to Damascus, my redemption. Yes, it had come late in my life, but nevertheless it had arrived when I least expected that such an event was even possible. The part that I had played in stopping Josh from killing Billy Tate, as conniving as it was, was also my act of mercy to someone who had taken from me the animal I loved, and harmed those who had taken me in when I was perilously close to death. Hannah was to say to me later, much later, in a quiet moment, that I had stopped the destruction of Josh's soul. That I don't know, but I knew that I had saved his life from the dark, depressing thoughts that come with killing. Well, at least for a while.

When I jerked Billy to his feet, not wishing to show any pity in case Josh should find me out, he began to beg for forgiveness. He must have still thought that his end was close. And as I dragged him to the barn he continued to whimper. Hannah followed and fetched a milking stool and motioned him to sit. He crumpled on to the seat, still in a panicked state, as Josh entered with a bucket and rags. Hannah undid the tie that held his wrist to his belt, but left the sling on his wounded arm and began to silently attend to his new wounds. She cleaned and dressed the cuts to face and ear in a methodical way and showed no sign of regard to the task. It was as if she were doing it to a stranger who had just then wandered into her life and who would then leave when fixed.

Billy sat mute, his eyes staring to some place not seen by the rest of us. He was in a state of shock and confusion and I am now sure that he thought I had not yet finished with him. His twitchy mannerisms were that of an animal looking to escape, so I had a feeling that he would run, and like Hannah, I was detached from any further concern or punishment, so didn't care anymore about Billy Tate. And that's what happened, he ran away that night and disappeared out of our lives. The only surprise was that he did it on his own two feet. If it had been me, I would have taken the horse.

It was Josh who carried the news to Hannah and myself the following morning by simply saying, 'He's gone.'

I went and looked and confirmed that it was true. He had gone, much like a passenger at a station, never to return. Was it the hand of the Lord seeking to make our lives better? If it was, then I didn't deserve such reparation but Hannah and Josh did.

I never dwelled on his fate, as it was not so much a mystery but rather just an occurrence with an unknown ending. Hannah asked, on just one occasion, would he return, and I just said, 'No.'

'How can you be sure?' she asked.

I told her that when men run away they don't come back to settle up. They may want to and they may think about it, constantly, letting it eat away at them, but their cowardice stops them from building the courage they need. When they go to act, all they can remember is their shame. Then I added,

'Especially the older they get,' and by then many years had passed.

The mending of the fence between Hannah, Josh and me was a slow affair. I secured the Emerson place but only after I had asked permission from the both of them. Hannah was neutral in her response, only saying that I should do what pleased me. I reminded her that if I did, we would be neighbours. Josh slept on his answer for two nights, before saying that it would be a pity to see the Emerson place fall into ruin as so much work had gone into the property. It was hardly a ringing endorsement but like a drowning man I was willing to clutch at any straw.

I told him I agreed and thanked him for his counsel.

When I moved in, it was not with the same buoyant heart I had experienced on my first visit. Dark thoughts debilitated me for some time and I had to force myself to stay off the bottle. So, in response, I worked like an indentured servant to wear my body out. And it worked, as routine and hard work can build a strong body and repair the spirit, but I must admit that there were times when I came close to ending it all, so I hid my handgun and rifle out in the barn cellar.

For the first five years, I made little contact with Hannah and Josh. When we did meet it was polite, but never more than that until Josh turned twenty. Out of the blue I received a written invitation, slipped under my door while working my few head of cattle up in the top pasture. It asked me to attend their Thanksgiving, which fell upon his birthday.

This offer had followed on from a chance meeting with Josh down on the river the previous week. We were both seeking a fish dinner and I had done well, but the fish were shy of his hook. I offered him half of my catch and he accepted and shook my hand with thanks. It was a strong grip from a fine young man. I asked after his mother, and did so in more than a passing gesture, and requested that he pass on my good wishes. Our conversation was short, but he did tell me that she was preparing for the holiday commemoration. However, he said nothing about any birthday celebration that was to be attached to that event.

I was touched with the receipt of the solicitation. However, when confronted with the realities of attending such an event, I hesitated. I tried to write back, saying that I was unable to attend, but each time I took the pen into my hand I knew that it was a lie. I had no excuses, only the shy fear of having to see and be near Hannah again. I therefore planned to attend, pay my respects, and quickly leave. But when I got there, Josh welcomed me with a warm smile that extended to his eyes.

I was not the only guest, thank the Lord, and the merriment of the occasion was helped along by two new neighbouring families, who had taken up land further down river. The happiness that comes from young children celebrating Thanksgiving and Josh's birthday was captivating, so I stayed and I'm glad I did. The food, the music and the company lightened my fearful heart.

I avoided Hannah that day, mixing with our neighbours who were part of a co-operative of families who had set up a steam sawmill in the valley. Just as I was ready to leave, I approached Hannah and stumbled over my words of thanks as I bid goodbye, while she smiled and touched the back of my hand. I still had a whole lot of guilt buried deep, but Hannah had no intention of digging up the past. She only wished to speak of the present and the future for Josh. Her understanding of life was large, while mine had remained small and solitary.

This brief encounter was more than a good start, as I would go on to see Hannah two or three times a year for the years that followed, drawing and living on each of those meetings until the next.

Some twelve years after the disappearance of Billy from our lives, an unexpected discovery was made up on the mountain in the summer of 1909. A professional photographer had hauled his heavy equipment up to the pass on the back of a mule, where he made camp before collecting images of nature for a geographic magazine. He had come over on to our side of the pass to take in the vista of the valley, and after he had taken his pictures and was ready to leave, he dropped his water canteen that skidded off a large smooth rock and down into a smaller rocky outcrop. When he went to retrieve the container, from where it had fallen out of sight, he made a grizzly find. It was a bag of bones, the skeletal remains of Billy Tate wrapped in the rags that were once his clothes. His leather belt with its brass buckle and his boots were still well preserved, and allowed me to confirm that it was Billy to the Deputy from Preston.

It seemed that he had tried to cross back over the pass and like me, he got lost. What his intentions were should he get to the safety of the other side, I don't know, but the early snows of that year caught him out. He was on foot, wounded and about three miles up on the ridge, and a mile north of the pass.

It is not known if he fell or wedged himself in between the rocks in a vain attempt to find shelter as none of his bones were found to be broken, but that's where he met his frozen death. It would have been a desperate and lonely end for any man, but particularly one so young and frightened. I can only hope that it was over quickly.

Josh took a wife the following year when he was twenty-seven. She was a girl from one of the mill families who was twenty-two years, and looked a lot like a young Hannah in stature, and even more so in manner as the years passed. They had three sons, the first two being born before Josh went off to the Great War in Europe at the age of thirty-four years. He was considered old for service even at that age, but his maturity and experience allowed him to quickly rise to the rank of Sergeant in General 'Black' Jack Pershing's army where he saw action at the Battle of Le Hamel. In that battle, he was wounded with shrapnel that left a mark just above the left eye that extended to the hairline. The metal fragment had come up under his helmet at lightning speed, but he was lucky, as were all of those young men who had survived those terrible battles.

On his return, Josh was full of stories of his travels to Paris and London, complete with photographs of fine young men standing next to motor vehicles of all shapes and sizes. He also showed me photographs of the battlefield weapons with artillery of a size that seemed impossible to comprehend, and of aeroplanes, large ones with two engines, and then there were the tanks. Giant metal beasts that went forward over the battlefield to breach and open the infantry lines. That man had progressed to such efficiency in destruction made my sins seem venial.

It was a little later, on my seventy-eighth birthday that Josh asked me about my time in the Civil War. I didn't wish to say very much, not because it was painful, but because I felt that my experiences of war would seem inconsequential to his. But as we spoke I realized that our experiences were common, just separated by some sixty years in time. We were just two akin soldiers, sitting together on my porch reminiscing, but our stories were not of daring and bravado. We spoke of the small things, the weariness, the cold, the poor food, the songs sung at night in the dark by men who desperately missed home. Then without knowing it, the conversation crossed to our personal feelings of the fears and the residue of war – of the men who had passed. Like a wave, I could feel the sentimentality of those years roll over me and the experiences came flooding back. The same seemed to be happening to Josh. Out of sight of all, on my porch and sitting on a swing bench and looking over the river, I reached out and held his hand, and together our tears fell in silence.

Josh wrote to me some weeks later, saying that a weight had been lifted from his shoulders. I wanted to reply and confide that it was I who had finally had that weight relieved after nearly a lifetime, but I was unable to do, so. However, I did write this story down as best I could and as honestly as I could. This is my small story, written in these school exercise books as a record, which I will place inside my trunk. My expectation is that Josh will discover them when he comes down to clean up my affairs after I have breathed my last. We have spoken of that time and he has told me that he will look after everything. I know he will. He is a man from good stock who was guided right and early by his father and forever more by his mother. And if somehow I have played some small part in the growth of his character, then my life has not been a waste.

While I don't expect this tale to mean much to anyone in particular, maybe, just maybe, Josh will pass these feeble words on to his sons, and in turn they will pass them on to their sons. If such an occurrence should happen and from these words they have learnt from my mistakes, then I will have left a legacy, and no man could want for more.

GMcD
1 June 1926